The following comments were in "real time" from readers of
November Novel, *by Assia Greene as the novel was being written;*
rather, as the novel was writing itself:

"...I'm reading Shasha's novel and I wonder how she does it—keeping details in her head—the torn jeans, Chaucer the dog, and those lonely, grief-stricken women...and I loved the ways that things showed up in unusual places, like the coffee mug from the coffee shop that wasn't even rebuilt yet."

"...just sat down and read all the excerpts...I'm not sure if I'm reading turns in your novel so much as turns in your mind. To put it another way, I'm starting to wonder if..."

"...hilarious how your thoughts are put into the form of dialogue or thinking that the characters are doing."

"You're three days behind on your word count?...Did I get this right—you refuse to write because you think something awful is about to happen to whom...?"

"...Totally nuts to see thoughts take form like that."

"...I'm dying to know where this explosion will lead!"

"I just finished reading your novel this morning...I hadn't run across a *manic tristesse* before. I especially enjoyed the way inanimate characters, such as the Golden Gate Bridge and the magic coffeepots insisted on having their share of the limelight. To call it Magical Realism... is to imply that it's..."

"[Magical Realism]...would never allow either Fate or the characters the freedom that you allow.... In your story nothing is foretold, or if it is, it's foretold incorrectly, such as Aesop's narrow escape on the 14th Street... But I know, at my age, that that's the way life goes: random events (and non-events that we don't notice)...somehow combine chaos with inevitability..."

"No one can write about the loneliness and grief we each endure, like you can."

"When are you sending the manuscript? I'm excited to read the full version instead of random excerpts that jump all over the place like an electron obeying quantum physics."

"So, we have Shasha writing November Novel about Assia who in turn is writing a November Novel and we can't tell whether Assia is a real fictional character, a facsimile of Shasha who has friends in her dimension, or has invented characters in a third dimension and do those characters begin to write her? And what dimension is Chaucer, the dog?...."

"...Then we have Violette, and I absolutely love the way the author, whoever she is, takes up the point of view of different characters—and how many degrees of pseudo-reality must we readers transcend? And that's the fascination...our minds so want to find the sense, the pattern that makes the outside world seem intelligible—whereas objective reality could be an illusion and in this case several dimensions of illusion."

"I adore the confusion. Can't wait to hear what happens next and at what level of unreality."

NOVEMBER NOVEL,
BY ASSIA GREENE

SHASHA C. CROCKETT

ISBN: 978-0-9882518-1-6

This is a work of fiction. Names, characters, places, and incidents are the products of the author's imagination or are used fictitiously. Any resemblance to actual events or persons, living or dead, is entirely coincidental.

Printed in the United States of America

Book Design by Patti Frazee

Dedication

For my November Novel writing partner, who is in November Novel writing his November Novel—as is the author of November Novel in the novel, writing hers alongside him—while coming to believe that she had no idea who was truly writing:

NOVEMBER NOVEL, BY ASSIA GREENE

Acknowledgments

Sincere gratitude is extended to the personnel and patrons of Spy House Coffee Shop and Dunn Bros Coffee Shop, in Minneapolis, for the windowed spaces, the lattes, the interest in, and the accompaniment for the writing of *November Novel by Assia Greene.*

TABLE OF CONTENTS

NOVEMBER NOVEL,
BY ASSIA GREENE

SHASHA C. CROCKETT

Everything vanishes around me, / and works are born as if out of the void. / Ripe, graphic fruits fall... / My hand has become the obedient instrument of a remote will.

—Paul Klee

All that is gold does not glitter, / Not all those who wander are lost; / The old that is strong does not wither, / Deep roots are not touched by the frost. / From the ashes a fire shall be woken, / A light from the shadows shall spring; / Renewed shall be blade that was broken, / The crownless again shall be king.

—J. R.R. Tolkien

Chapter I.

GREEN

"Here," Nate said. "Over here. I think that's for me. Have any half-and-half?—Sugar? I need plenty of sugar—Celie, I'm listening—justaminute... What's this thing about?—This... coffeepot. Seems to have a cord. What? Am I supposed to plug it in and brew my own? Can't figure this out..."

November 3, 2008

"Well," she said to him, as though he'd asked a question—and perhaps he had—"It's because November makes me fucking nuts."

She liked that as a first line for the novel she was attempting. She thought she might offend certain potential readers of her November Novel, jumping in like that—with a derivative of the word *fuck* gracing her first sentence. Apt, though. That's why she was writing. One-thousand-seven-hundred-words-per-day that she would fall into, instead of into her raw core being.

"NaNoWriMo"—National Novel Writing Month: November: The month of the year when an unwieldy and scattered conglomerate of duly registered, logged-in, blogged-on, would-be writers—throughout the United States, and in countries far and wide—attempted the 1667 words per day; a 50,000 word-count goal in the form of what for many might amount to a "schlocky" novel, perhaps—but a novel, nonetheless. The start date: November 1; ending time and date for the logged-in 50,000 words: midnight, November 30.

She'd begin, Like This: with this first character—the one already sitting across from her.

"Aesop—Aesop Wind-Rivers," he said, extending his hand to hers.

"Assia... Greene," she said, shaking his hand.

What an unusual and beautiful name this character has arrived with, Assia thought. Assia—the author, that is—of *November Novel.*

"D'you mind my language?" she said. "That... November making me—"

"Not at all. With enough hot coffee I can tolerate most things," Aesop said.

The coffee shop they were sitting in, was—*what?* Assia thought... *Crowded?—Nearly empty?* The setting eluded her. She'd ignore it for the moment. *Aesop is such an old name,* she thought. *A name that hasn't come back 'round again, yet.* While her name was a problem. People automatically saw *Asia in Assia,* or pronounced the first "a" in her name as if it sounded like the "a" in apple, when it was more the sound of the "a" in wash.

"Your name—'Assia'—the letters, that is—reminds me of the name 'Shissai'—the philosopher. D'you know of his writings?" Aesop said. "'*The warrior must only take care that his spirit is never broken...*' One of his lines. It's stuck with me. Always liked that one."

Assia glanced at him. His eyes—dark, into night-sky's deepest-blue. Luminous, like his straight dark hair tied in a ponytail and trailing down the back of his faded-out gray GRATEFUL DEAD T-shirt.

"I have no plot, you know," she said, "which is—in theory, at least—not a problem for the November Novel; 'No Plot No Problem' seems to be the motto for November Novel. I don't write fiction—can't imagine where my characters, or setting—y'know, those sorts of elements that are supposedly supposed to be part of a novel—where they'll come from. But I'm committed to it, Aesop. For one thing, I have to write myself through November. November drags me to despair... I think I already said that."

3

Aesop poured coffee from the pot on the table, one of the always too-small tables that are the norm in coffee shops most of the world over, an exception being France—where the tables are even smaller. He lifted the pot toward Assia, quirking his eyebrow in unspoken question.

Assia shook her head: "No. Thanks. I got a good start on caffeine with a double espresso I picked up at a street vendor's while walking here this morning."

Assia didn't know where the coffeepot had come from. *There are never actual pots on the tables in coffee shops.* This one was silver, a glass knob on its top affording sight of the

coffee *blurking* against the glass, the coffee's color darkening as it perked. The pot had a cord trailing from its side, winding over the table's edge. Assia leaned over the side of the table, peering beneath, to see if she could determine where the cord was plugged in. She could see the cord hanging loose, and no outlet in sight.

"Aesop, did you bring that coffeepot?"

Aesop shook his head. "I don't think so."

She could understand that—that not knowing. She felt rather *vague* herself. Mystified. As though a fog, barely beginning to burn off, shrouded the setting. She could ascertain tables, and people started to form into view—*someone lifting a package from a chair, a woman staring into space, thinking—sitting across from someone—a man—who seemed agitated. He wanted something— what was it?*

Something gold—attached to... what?

Something that glittered.

Someone wandering.

Something lost—a woman, gold-red hair trailing wisps over her forehead—*looking for something. What was she looking for?*

Violette slid her chair back, and bending down, looked under the table. "What happened to the package I had here? Those jeans... I couldn't've put it too far from my backpack. I don't see it though. Hmmm..."

And then, something... Ashes! That was it! Floating... Why would that be? Assia could even hear, from the outside of the shop, *a dog barking, insistently.*

Something... broken.

Chaucer suddenly, again, leapt at the window, this time hitting the glass with such force that the small panes of the coffee shop window looked as though they would give way. Every head turned. Violette screamed, "Chaucer!"

She smelled the scent of... what? *Something... driftingly sweet. What was it? Something like...*

It fell. Kept falling. Like the rain. Dust, debris, blood, the smell of damp and wet, and... roses.

But Assia had merely a misted sense of that which was around her—*not unlike coming to consciousness through layers of anesthesia,* she thought. She looked around hoping to ground herself in something, tried to see if other tables had coffeepots on them. Didn't see any. Assia shrugged. *Maybe setting isn't my thing.*

"I've got somewhere near one-thousand words to do yet, today, Aesop—to meet my seventeen-hundred words-per-day quota. Although it's more challenging than that—I'm some days late starting this November Novel," she said. "D'you think it's okay if I don't get much beyond the first couple of pages, for day... three?"

"No problem," Aesop said.

She noted Aesop had no newspaper, nor anything to read, actually. A newspaper might've given her a clue about setting. Just his coffee. *How is it the coffee perks, when the pot isn't plugged in?* Aesop was staring into the steam's wafting, drifting over his mug of coffee. Focusing intently, with a studied consideration that was indecipherable to Assia. Assia turned her head to look out the window. *A window... Wait. Is there a window?* She looked around the room, adjusted the bracelets twining around her upper arm, and pushed her brown hair, tangling, from her shoulder.

—the woman, her light brown hair tangling over a pale yellow, velvety shirt—red stitching criss-crossing... bracelets high on her arm, interspersed with... glittering—twined... amidst... Jeweled earrings... refracted sunlight—streaming— through the large, multi-paned front window by their table—leaded glass splintering chaotic light against the walls of the crowded coffee shop.

Yes! She could see it now—a large, multi-paned window beside their table, streaming full morning sun over them, glancing bright glistened light off the silver coffeepot. She shaded her eyes with her hand, her sapphire earrings sparkling and looked out. Looked to be an urban sort of street. Assia sighed. *That's a relief. I don't want to feel morose, with my novel in a setting that connotes small town loneliness.* And with that bias put squarely out there, she thought she might have lost another set of readers, or at least offended them.

"Doesn't something need to happen, Aesop?" she asked, "so the story can start?"

Warning signals blinked, adamantly—scattering ominous orange hues over emergency vehicles parked at odd angles up and down the street. On the tops of squad cars, sirens flashed, spinning— throwing red light wildly arcing—radios squawked. The rain fell, incessantly. Unrelenting...

"What the hell happened?"

"Wasn't it Joseph Heller, whose book was titled *Something Happened*? Something needs to happen. I can't understand how fiction could possibly work."

She spied the stack of paper on the table in front of Aesop. Pale blue. A ream. Not that she knew how many pieces of paper constituted a ream; writer that she was, and therefore should know that bit of information, it would seem—those sorts of details did not stick with her. Other sorts of details stuck with her, instead. Less practical ones. It was simply the descriptor that came to mind when she looked at the stack of pale blue papers and that was enough for Assia. Aesop poured more coffee from the pot, steam scouting smokelike over the table.

"Hmmm... I love the smell of coffee," Assia said. "Sometimes I suspect that's all I like about it—the smell. Just the thought of coffee perks me up—no pun intended. I don't understand this coffeepot setup. Shouldn't it be plugged in, somehow—to keep the coffee warm?"

Nate stopped typing, sank back in his chair, and ran his fingers through his hair, pushing it back, and away from his eyes.

"Why does that guy have coffee in a regular cup and I have this infernal pot-thing trying to perk itself into something? Can't understand it. Excuse me, where'd you get that coffee?"

Assia looked at Aesop, lifted an eyebrow. "Aesop, what is your work?"

"I'm an antagonist."

"Really! Well... what does an antagonist do? I know what an antagonist is in a novel, for example, but in one's real life... It sounds rather negative. Wouldn't you rather be a protagonist?"

Aesop lifted his fingers slightly from the computer keyboard in front of him, seemed to give Assia's question some thought. *Where'd the keyboard come from?* She hadn't noticed it. *Why the 'ream' of blank paper, if the keyboard?* Aesop shifted in his chair, set the coffeepot nearer the edge of the table, and stacked his papers—blue-upon-blue, tapping the edges into place on the surface of the table. "Let's go," he said. "It's Time. Check your word count—see how close you are to your 1700 words for today."

Assia flipped over to "tools" and "word count" on her laptop. "Ah, the little rectangle shows me the word 'close'!"

"I think that means close, as in 'open' or 'close,' but perhaps I've been wrong about that all along. Close is close enough. You've made a start." Aesop reached for his backpack on the floor, and slung it over his shoulder. "I've an idea where we're going today. I love a day, just... Like This." Assia put her laptop in her bag. "Do we take the pot with us?" she asked.

Chapter II.

VIOLET

Violette watched the two gathering their things in preparation to leave. The woman, her light brown hair tangling over a pale yellow, velvety shirt—red stitching criss-crossing the neckline. Beaded bracelets—interspersed with tiny gems, glittering—twined around her upper arm—emerald, amethyst, gold topaz—amidst turquoise beads. The colours entranced—Violette's seamstress eye caught each detail. Jeweled earrings of light sky blue refracted sunlight streaming through the large, multi-paned front window by their table—leaded glass splintering chaotic light against the walls of the crowded coffee shop. As the two stood to leave, Violette saw the woman's faded-to-colour-washed-indigo jeans, and her well-worn hiking boots. The man was lanky, intelligent looking—*Though how would I know that?* she thought... *Gentle seeming, in an "otherworldly"* way—she didn't know how else to describe it. Hair like ink.

The yin and the yang—these two. She couldn't guess the relationship, quite. There was the way they'd met one another's gaze—so straight on. *The way they'd touched one another as if— as if, what?* As if they'd known one another across something—and didn't know it.

> **They hold one another's arms, her fingers around his forearm, his around hers. Across... wreckage... that they've found floating in the water. Or maybe it found them.**

The way the woman had laid her hand alongside his forearm and he'd placed his along hers—across the table.

She'd never seen pants like those the man was wearing—leather—canvas-coloured. Unusual, yet they looked right, on him. Violette had tried to get a view to see if the pants had fringe scattering along the seams, which she'd half-expected. The woman was somewhat compelling. She realized it sounded strange to put "somewhat" and "compelling" together like that, but it's how she felt. She was drawn to the woman, yet sensed that if she got too close she could fall... into that woman's life.

Violette decided to have a go at the coffeepot on their now-vacated table. She could see the end of the cord, dangling, and wondered if it was not within reach of a plug-in. There were cords strung along the floor, hither and yon, the coffee shop patrons re-charging laptops. This month, the coffee shop was filled with those settling in to work on their November Novels. The only real reason she knew about November Novel was that Celia, her closest friend, was starting it for the first time and had told her about it. For Violette, the coffee shop was a haven. Home felt crowded for her—with friends or neighbors stopping by unannounced, often staying through meal-times. The company of strangers in public places distracted her less.

Violette picked up the silver coffeepot. *Ah... there's coffee in it, yet. Odd that it seems full. I'm sure I saw the man refill his coffee mug a few times, at the least, while I was yet watching.* She spied an outlet near an adjacent table and moved the pot, settling it near enough to the available outlet. Violette wiggled the plug-in into the outlet, and pulled a chair up to the table. She sat, settling her chin in her hands, elbows on the table, waiting... *Luck! This will get the coffee perking in no time—not that I want any. I only want to watch it.* Within seconds the pot *sizzed*—the auditory response she was hoping for. Violette quickly glanced 'round to see if the sound had bothered anyone. *People are mulling over their work all over this place today—looks like every table is taken, save this one,* someone already having set their things on the table Violette had vacated. Coffee cooled in thick coffee mugs, beside tapping fingers. *These coffee shops would be better named writers' markets*, she thought.

The now-hissing *ssssst* drew Violette. She watched the glassed-knob top carefully, recalling that it'd take a bit of time for anything to appear. Violette remembered her grandmother's coffeepot with the same clear glass knob on the top of the lid. She'd watch it... Like This. That grandmother, Grandmother Fiona—with the coffeepot—was the grandmother she was *not* named for, having been named for the one she hardly saw. Her middle name, Vanessa, was for Grandmother Violette's twin sister: Violette Vanessa McEwen. Plenty-a-name for a small child. Violette felt she was barely coming into the name. She didn't mind it, at all. She liked the colour violet, even; yet, *violet* connoted a fragility she was oft-times not attuned with. She knew herself to be buoyed with an inner strength that sustained her, though she understood that people could see her as *waiflike*. She figured that was because of the watery mist of missing, encircling her so much of the time. When did the missing start? *Sometimes I feel I was born with this feeling—a feeling of looking for someone—not understanding why. Maybe I was supposed to have been a twin. Like Francesca and Jessamine, these daughters of mine, coming into the world with one another.*

There were times Violette felt a golden essence filling the core of her, expanding through her center, painting itself upward and into her heart—infusing calm centeredness. Colour. Grounding energy. She wasn't sure how to describe it other than that she felt *accompanied*—that she was not alone with the vulnerability and fear, recurring, that swept through her—body and senses.

At times, the colour left her inner body, swirling in protective aura around her. She felt connected—as if by umbilical cord—

to something both primal, and universal. A force benevolent, reassuring. *All will be well.* But there were times, Like This, when the arc—the spiral that was life experiencing itself, through her—time-traveled itself and wound 'round too close to her deepest griefs. When that intersection dissolved into being, she saw herself like a cricket—an unappealing image, but it was how she felt—jumpy as all hell, with a fragile cracking shell. Empty inside. Certainly, insects were not "empty"—but her image of herself at those times, was.

Grief. She'd left her home in England, for California, where her son Eli was in college—to help him navigate post-surgery recovery from a serious knee injury. A trauma that in retrospect was nothing, nothing at all in the broader arc of what was to come. Eli's knee had been ensconced in a full-leg cast. He'd been unable to manage the pain, even with medications. Or to walk, even with the aid of crutches. Violette had been beside herself with helplessness; parental love—inextricably bound with a vulnerability that is simply too much to ask. Too much for anyone.

She'd felt powerless to know what to do for this child, Eli—his first year away from home; so unbelievably far away, injured beyond her understanding. She, having just separated from his father. Violette felt lost—and found, as well, in other ways, simultaneously. She'd had to remind herself whenever the panic washed through her Like This, that she'd been alone all along, in the marriage, anyway.

She found herself sitting on the tiny, wrought-iron balcony that she'd glimpsed through French doors, at the end of the long hallway that ran arrow-straight, bisecting the row of fourth floor dorm rooms. Eli's bed had been moved from his fourth-floor dorm room to a room on the main level—the better to accommodate his immobility. She'd come to this uppermost floor of the dorm to gather Eli's books and clothes, and had found herself drawn to the balcony—hoping to catch some air in the hundred-degree heat.

She was aware of the near coolness of the ironwork railing of the balcony. Exhaustion, fueled by worry for her son, wound through her like a leveling wind. Settled into the snug balcony-space, she lifted her hair from the back of her neck, and blew her breath upward over her face. She remembers looking over the edge. I could lean; I could fall over this edge. *Not that she'd ever do anything like that. Of course. It was the sense of leaning, something she longed to do at that moment. Leaning into someone who could take it. Like Celia, for instance—this longtime best friend of hers. Violette pulled herself back from the edge.* What I would ever do without Celia, I can't begin to imagine.

And though it had seemed to her that her son, Eli, had come into this world with his name in place, it was years later—when, exactly, she couldn't recall—that she'd noticed his name contained within that of her closest friend, as though she'd lifted "Eli" from the center of Celia.

Eli had been emergently able on his crutches when she'd left him, finally, to return to England. Yet, when meeting Eli's plane on an early summer's evening, Violette had not been prepared to see her beloved child, nineteen-years-old that past spring, limping as he walked toward her, an image that would intrude again and again in her mind's eye. No way to explain it to anyone, her inability to assimilate that image. Anyone that is, except other parents who welcomed sons home—from war, or any number of possibilities of experiences—in a less than whole way, in the ways any parent innocently takes for granted their children will be whole.

Violette looked at the coffeepot, impatient for the darkening coffee to begin to jump into the glassed top—remembering then, that she'd agreed to meet Celia around lunchtime. She retrieved her backpack from its spot on a vacated chair, tempted to put her cheek into the buttery feel of the leather—worn to smooth—just the way she'd wanted it to be, the way leather was meant to be worn in. But she thought if she did that, it could be the break in the levee holding back her tears. Tears in coffee shops Like This didn't raise an eyebrow, amongst the writers, students, and what-have-you, but she knew that, in her case, tears would segue to sobs.

She needed to be on her way. Violette gathered her things and prepared to step outside to the patiently waiting Chaucer, his gold leash looped around the ironwork of the bicycle rack in front of the shop. She turned to look back at the table, tapped her chin in thought. *Should I leave the coffeepot plugged in?*

CHAPTER III.
SLATE/ RUST

Assia had thought it sunny when she'd looked out the windows of the coffee shop as she and Aesop had prepared to leave—but clearly, it was not. The sun had clouded over, and the air was cool as they meandered along the walkways to the river. Assia pulled her sweatshirt closer, zipping it, and adjusted the backpack on her shoulders.

"Aesop, let's not go to the river yet," she said. "I'm afraid I'll lose you to the river. That you'll fall in, vanish." Aesop looked at her, reached his hand toward her face, pushed her hair from her forehead—an affectionate gesture she loved.

"Maybe I can just write you into permanence. Can I do that, d'you think? *Do I need something to be permanent?* Yes! I do! I understand all about 'letting go' and 'letting be'—breathing, impermanence. Zen. Attachment and yearning, and the 'wanting mind.' I have that, Aesop—the 'wanting mind.' I don't want to accept impermanence. I think it's unfair to ask of any of us. But what could the alternative possibly be? The whole physics of things needs to change. Or I need to." Assia bent down to tie her bootlace. For an instant—the tiniest moment—she felt relief.

Violette's plan was to get a running start on her painting, before meeting Celia. Chaucer scampered and jumped excitedly—a mode that Violette was learning as typical for the dog. Violette was barely getting used to having a pet at all, let alone trying to understand Chaucer in particular. She'd somehow retained custody of the dog when she'd separated from her relationship with Stephen, Chaucer's owner. Violette loved Chaucer's colouring—tan and beige, vanillalike—like the pants the man in the coffee shop was wearing. Similar in colour, and of like softness, she imagined.

Violette pulled her sweater around her, buttoned it against

the damp and the growing coolness. She put her face into the fur of Chaucer's neck for an instant and sighed. "Let's go, my friend," she said. She shrugged her backpack over her shoulders, tucked the bag that held her painting easel under her arm, and wound the end of Chaucer's gold leash around her hand.

She thought the Thames would be the place to paint, although she was hesitant to set up her easel with the sky so near to misting. *I need a warmer climate. I so dislike being cold, or damp—but that is truly the essence of England's fall-into-winter.* Violette shifted her bag more snugly under her arm. *Yet, I don't want to be away from England in the fall, with the rains holding an easy steadiness*—yellows, reds, and golds drawing her eyes downward in the autumn's damp while she walked over painted-wet leaves. When she'd been in America, in the fall, the season had passed in a weekend—or so it had seemed. But she'd soaked it in—California's warmth—painting outside under the sun's knowing gaze.

Violette painted for herself, alone, often experiencing paintings coming through her, without prompting—from where, she didn't know. Sometimes people stopped to purchase her work, and she was happy enough just to hand a painting over for the Pounds, Euros, or Dollars. If she thought she could make her living as a painter, she would. She could, perhaps, rearrange her life to do just that. But then, Simon wanted her to earn a decent living, so they could continue to afford their brownstone in the city. She wasn't sure how long Simon would be in her life. She pulled inward, thinking. She'd never let herself say that aloud to anyone—her thinking about leaving Simon. Maybe she'd said it to Celia. Once, maybe. She felt the tears then, unbidden, as Chaucer bounded ahead, yanking her arm. She pushed the heel of her other hand onto her cheek to stop the slip of tears, the easel starting to slide from beneath her arm. *Oh, for a place to cry.* Home was busy, people about, always. And London as well, of course. She lifted the bag from her shoulders, readjusting it, put the easel more snugly in place and wound Chaucer's gold leash an extra loop around her hand.

Assia and Aesop walked along HORSE GUARD'S PARADE turning left toward PARLIAMENT SQUARE.

"I'm enchanted with the names of these walkways and streets. The one we saw the other day—'BIRD CAGE WALK'— what d'you think that name means, E?"

"Haven't a clue," Aesop said.

They stopped for a moment, inhaling Westminster Abbey. Something they did, reflexively, each time they caught view of it. An ache of dis-ease—ancient—wafted through Assia, catching her breath. "E," Assia said, reaching for his hand. "How lonely can a *soul* be, on this planet? How lonely can a person be, and still be alive, E? "

"Assia," he said, looking at her. He didn't carry the loneliness she did, but he knew hers, because he knew her. It hadn't taken him long to sense it in her, though he didn't consider himself particularly intuitive. Maybe loneliness was evident when that encompassing.

Assia drew her breath in, deeply—hoping it would reach that so tightly held place in her. *What is it that's being held so?* she wondered, unable to find words to put to it. "Can't contain it all, some days, E," she said. "... don't know what to do about it. It's so fucking big—doesn't seem like a person ought to have to hold it all, Like This." She pulled herself into stillness, not moving for several heartbeats, as though that might be antidote enough. Holding On. When it settled into her Like This, she was safe from loneliness nowhere, even in the light of day. Even with Aesop. She didn't want to drown him with her lost-nesses. She didn't want to be "that" with him—a person that lonely.

They made their way toward the Thames. She'd always pictured the River Thames as muddy brown, like the Mississippi River of her childhood wanderings, but the Thames surprised her with its slate-blueness. Stepping around people and their dogs, Aesop and Assia sat on a bench along the wide walkway, the magnificent Houses of Parliament in view. It was early, yet there were many people about, walking to work, or trailing behind dogs pulling ardently at leashes. Assia loved that about an urban-scape—people everywhere—seemed to ease the empty spaces inside her, as though she could fill herself with things external. She couldn't grasp the concept of filling herself from within, or more so than that, tapping into a great eternal fullness. She'd never tapped it.

She and Aesop planned to take the train up to Cambridge that afternoon. Aesop hoped to access the Cambridge University libraries, to peruse manuscripts from 16th century sources that he'd been unable to find anywhere else; hoping for some inroads in his work providing consultation on a Native American law case, his area of expertise. It was the reason he and Assia had come to London. Galloway and Porter Bookstore on Sidney Street would be their first stop. Assia knew of the bookstore from her Cambridge University days, and a colleague in Aesop's law firm had recommended it to him.

Assia was eager to see Cambridge again. She'd been on a summer study program, and the Michaelmas term—stretching from the first of October, to just past mid-December—at Cambridge University, as an undergraduate. She wanted, once again, to see the boats punting on the River Cam along the banks of King's College, and to gaze at the majestic Gothic architectural spires of King's College Chapel. Assia was counting on the chapel being open to visitors—to enter its cavernous space, tip her head back and look up and up, and yet further upward, sending her awe into the fan-vaulted ceilings.

Aesop had wandered over to look at a painting set on an easel along the wide walkway that bordered the Thames. A woman was painting with broad, concentrated strokes, her cocker spaniel at her feet. Assia gathered her backpack and, stepping around leashes wound around benches, walked toward the space just off the main walkway where the woman was working.

The artist was holding a paint tube above her palette, eyes on the paint oozing from the tube onto the surface of her palette. She tossed the paint tube aside and reached for her brush in one motion, without taking eyes from the palette. She tapped the paintbrush into the oils, arrayed like jewels.

Assia tipped her head, studying the painting from this bit of distance. The painting looked nothing like the Thames, or the Houses of Parliament in view here. For Assia, at first glance, it evoked the Golden Gate Bridge. *Why would that be?* She stepped closer.

Violette noted the pant legs first—the man from the coffee shop she'd been intrigued with. She glanced down at Chaucer as the two meandered closer. Chaucer didn't stir, an unusual-for-him, quieted state. Violette turned toward the woman—Green. Her eyes. Like Celia's—darker, though, in colouration. Something about her... Violette felt an echo deep in her body—like a heart

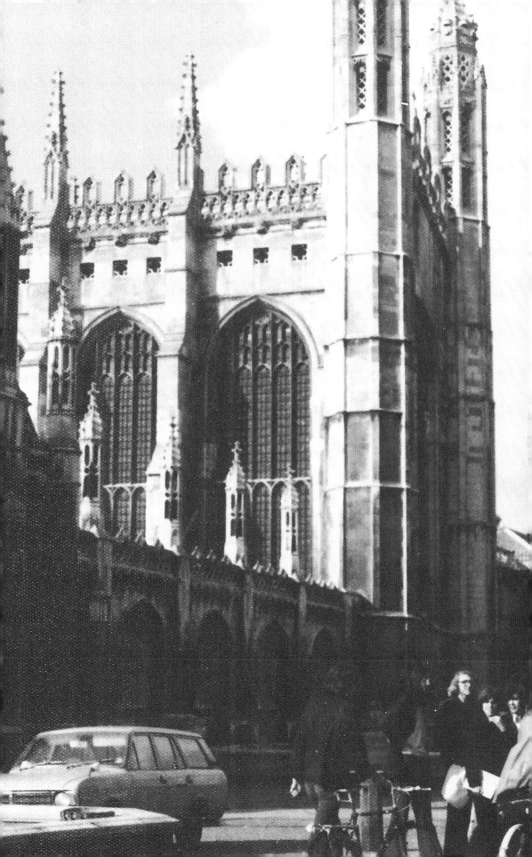

murmur. This woman seemed to carry deep feeling. Someone had once told Violette that she was tuned to a high intuitive harmonic... sensing dimensions hidden to most. Violette could see that this woman was not carrying this well of deep feeling, comfortably. *Who could, really?* Violette understood that—all too clearly—but she didn't fall to those depths, anymore. Not again. At least, she hoped. Violette sighed, and brushed a stray curl from her forehead.

Violette swept a gold-red arc of rich oil paint onto the canvas; glancing skyward, she willed the sun to come from behind one particular cloud to warm her. She liked to paint without the least bit of chill in the air, but the temperature was not accommodating. She could easily recall the exact orange-red of the Golden Gate Bridge. Rust running to gold—sun and blood. She needed only to mix her paints suitably to find it. *Odd, this—standing in front of the Houses of Parliament, the Thames, these people behind me on benches, studiously focused on their newspapers... What is it that's all over the papers, lately? Oh, yes... the upcoming American elections—Of course! All of this having nothing to do with the Golden Gate Bridge, yet, something about it all seems to be just what I need to get those San Francisco Bay colours...*

Aesop pulled off his jacket, tossing it to the edge of the walkway behind him. Violette noticed the graphic on his T-shirt: GRATEFUL DEAD. She paused, set her brush on the tray of the easel, tipped her head to the side, and tapped her chin—

What was that GRATEFUL DEAD song?... the one Neal played when we drove along the Bay Bridge through the morning fog... Neal loved the GRATEFUL DEAD. The Bay fog... I miss it. She picked up her brush again and swirled it in the paint, eyebrows drawn in thought. *What is it about the GRATEFUL DEAD that sets Simon off so? That British thing about American rock music, I suppose. Hard to say with Simon. "takes the wheel when I'm seein' double/ pays my ticket when I speed." That title simply escapes me... Magnolia something...*

CHAPTER IV.
FLAXEN/ GOLD

Celia was agitated. She'd decided to work from home for the morning, trying to get through the beginning stages of her project for the newest art installation at the Tate, hoping to meet Violette at the gallery by 1:00. She wanted Violette to look at the painting, *Departing in Yellow*, with her. She was taken with Alber's paintings of squares in colour variations. Never could decide on her favorite, though the brightly designed *Departing in Yellow* was the one that her mind returned to, over and again. It was not part of the current displays at the Tate, but the curator had said he'd unlock the storage area for her, to give her the opportunity to get a close look at it.

Celia had a print of the painting that she'd picked up from the frame shop a week ago. It was still on the floor of her living room, leaning against the wall. She hadn't figured the best place for it. Yet, that is. She'd noticed that the morning sunlight, slanting through the east living room windows, threw a triangle of light over the print, just where it was, propped along the windowed wall—a triangle of gold light, precisely bordering the innermost square. The serendipitous play of light was something she'd wanted to preserve, and had thereby not moved the print from its happenstance position.

The painting had four squares, as Celia saw it: the outer square, which was actually a perimeter, light brown in tone, calling to mind, for Celia, the scent of cinnamon. Next, a golden topaz, bordering a colour the very one of the butterscotch candies her grandmother had kept in the tall green glass jar on her kitchen counter. The innermost square, flaxen. The painting seemed to move "out-to-in," truly *departing* into the yellow center. She'd had a yellow falling-apart Fiat, before trading it in on her now-faded turquoise-green MINI, and had liked thinking she was *departing in yellow* each morning as she left for work.

Anxiety jumped, dispiriting Celia, as she prepared to leave her flat for the Tate. It wasn't her work at the Tate Gallery that was discomfiting; she relished the independence—trust, really— that she'd quite readily been granted in designing programs and exhibits for the public. It was leaving her solitude—that's where the anxiety stepped in and, as if looking around and spying a comfortable chair, made itself at home—agitating Celia's state-of-being—a state that was a rather tenuous peace in the best of circumstances lately.

Celia knew she needed to engage with the world. It was just far nicer to stay in—solaced, in her green silk dressing gown— the gown that she'd, by happenstance, come across in a small vintage Shoppe along an alleyway by Westminster Abbey. Celia did not typically take interest in vintage clothing, but the name of the tiny storefront had caught her eye: *Dante's Muse*—

She'd found herself turning into the Shoppe, stepping from the narrow alley-way into the dimmed light of the tiny space, scented with tea rose. As her eyes grew accustomed to the change in light, Celia's gaze magnetized to green—a deep vine-green colour of... a dress, was it? *Perhaps a dressing gown?* She couldn't tell. The flowing green fabric was ensconced amongst a mishmash of clothing items. Celia pulled it from the unwieldy, wiggly rack; she set it atop the rack and stepped back to disentangle her small purse from her shoulder and its crisscross over the front of her jersey. Celia slipped the gown over her jersey, eschewing dressing rooms at all costs, no matter—she never went in them—and she doubted the existence of a dressing room of any sort at all, in this tiny charming enclave. This would do. She was less attenuated to the fit, as it was; it was the particular shade of green she'd been drawn to. This... *connendula*—the only name she could come up with for it—draped over her shoulders, fell at her waist, and dropped to the floor. The sensory drift of green satisfied something in her.

She'd purchased the gown on the spot. For its colour, of course. Though usually quite circumspect about acquiring things, now and again Celia bought something based on what she'd come to call an *intuitive insistence*. Celia recalled nothing else about the Shoppe and had, indeed, been unable to find it when curious to have another look. When she'd inquired, no one seemed to have heard of it.

What Celia most wanted was to tuck-in, to write. Her personal writing aside, she was trying to get a jump start on her November Novel. Working at the Tate, full days, did not leave her time nor energy enough. She'd thought she could perhaps gain extra writing time in the mornings, yet had found that even arising an hour to two earlier than per-usual did not accommodate that goal; she'd, instead, luxuriated in the extra time—opening the flat, making a pot of tea and adjusting the blinds on the windows such that the light coming into her flat would be exactly right when she returned in the early evening.

Celia sighed. *Ah, this November Novel... I truly think I "might could" distract myself from these frustrations. Hold on—that's not the word. This... distress, rather, about the... Well, what would it be? Untenable—that seems right—untenable situations in my life—if I could either lose my mind, so to speak, in these 1700 words a day I need to write—or write some of the distressful wanderings into the words. Actually, I sometimes feel I've, indeed, already lost my mind. Maybe there's a chance I could catch hold of another. Fiction... Can't imagine writing fiction. How shall I commence starting? It is clear that I need to begin... somehow. The coffee shop on the corner at St. James Park looks to be a chosen spot for those working on this November Novel. I could meet Nate there, to write. Perhaps tomorrow.*

I wonder if it's time to give notice at the Tate—see what I could manage, freelancing... Take the leap of faith. Which would not be a leap into darkness! I will not let myself think that way!

Celia grabbed pen and a scrap of paper from the kitchen drawer beside the sink. She turned off the electric kettle. While pouring hot water over the Jasmine tea leaves, she wrote: *"Call J., re. finances"* on the paper scrap, anchoring it to the counter with a pottery mug. She'd call her financial planner, later—and figure how to manage leaving this job. *Is that an actual possibility?* Celia wondered. *Of course it is. It just depends on the variables. That's what I'll tell him.* Celia readied herself for leaving; drawing her hair back into a silken headband, she gathered her work satchel, took a quick sip of tea and locked the door of her flat behind her—all while lost in thought.

Assia contemplated. She ran her fingers through her hair lifting it back over her shoulder. "E, let's see if we can buy this painting. The light in it catches me. What d'you think?" Aesop, bent down on one knee, was scratching Chaucer's ears and neck. The dog sat up, wriggling delightedly. "Sure," Aesop said, distracted. "Whatever you want, Assh."

Assia approached the painter-artist, hesitating as she saw

the woman concentrating, mixing oils on the palette and then on the canvas. Violette, pressing brush to canvas, blending the oils, looked over at this interesting-looking woman approaching, and smiled. She liked the worn sweatshirt—zipped, over the yellow shirt—liked her ripped denims. *Only an American would wear clothing like that in public,* she thought. *More threads than denim, those pants—a truly crazed, threaded-holding-together*—a visual metaphor for Violette for the horrific phase in her life when she'd felt more "threaded," than "fabric-ed,"—feelings she intuited that this woman was shadowed by. It echoed in Violette—the place of despair, the likes of which she hoped never to visit again. There was, though, Violette thought, a certain freedom inherent in jeans like that—breathing spaces, intrigue, *mystery*—fragility that's held in some way. That sense of not knowing what, nor how, nor where—nor when—needing to have faith, instead. In something. Yet, Violette had had none of that faith. Grief had had its way with her, pulling her to stillness-unto-dread, weighting her—holding her sleep hostage, at night. In the mornings, awakening to the conscious realization of loss. The state of being that was of *lossnessing—accessing nothing, save loss.*

Assia stepped closer, engaging Violette's attention, "Your painting... is remarkably reminiscent for me of things American. I'm not quite sure why that would be," Assia said. "The Golden Gate Bridge, actually. That's what I see in it... I'm missing America—so much right now. Well, I suppose I'm missing many things. Too many. No matter. This painting of yours... I wonder... Is it okay if I take a closer look?"

Aesop stood up to give the excited Chaucer a chance to settle himself. Stepping closer to Assia, he stood behind her and put his arms around her, containing her in his loose embrace. He reached to the waistband of her jeans and threaded his index finger through the rip in the front of Assia's jeans, running his finger over the silken skin of her thigh; all the while, Assia was talking to the beautiful woman with paintbrush in hand, gold paint dripping onto the canvas—she, not watching, nor seeming to care—her eyes on Assia. The artist-woman's hair was swept in a loose tangle, gold-red trailing wisps lifting over her face.

What's that French word? Aesop thought, his eyes on Violette, as she turned toward Assia. "*Echevelé*"... *Is that it?... The sense of things coming... slightly undone.* A state that Aesop recalled liking. The painting itself, clearly barely begun, looked vaguely *en désordre*, as well... more so, with the gold paint unattended to, echoing over the canvas. Aesop couldn't ascertain the process of this painting—what was happening with it—yet Assia was already sure she wanted to buy it. For the life of him, Aesop could not see what it was about the painting-in-process that seemed to call to one's senses the Golden Gate Bridge, though he had to admit that something in the composition of these broadest brush strokes had called forth that vision. Close as he was, Aesop could not decipher the conversation between the artist and Assia. Aesop turned his gaze, taking in the until-now un-noted awareness of the public around them—the folks out-and-about on the walkways, people reading on the nearby benches.

There's an intimate connect, Aesop thought—*a certain, specific kind of intimacy that can occur within the private-amidst-public spaces. No intention of notice, and the nearly unconscious awareness of surrounding public venue.* If these business-type folks on the benches, reading the *London Times* with such studied concentration, happened to glance their way, Aesop paid them no mind.

Assia turned slightly. Aesop's finger wandered over the front of her thigh. For an instant, he truly wished they were alone. He'd managed to get two fingers, now, into the ripped tear, pulling at the threads stitching denim-to-denim together as haphazardly as Assia's words to him in those late-at-night phone calls, when he wasn't there and she missed him. He loved her missing. No one could miss like Assia could. Aesop knew that Assia's missing came with the depth of her lost places, and he was so sorry such sweetest falling had come at this very cost.

"I'm quite taken with your painting," Assia said. "Would you consider selling it to me?"

Violette couldn't think to sell the painting in its current state of incompletion. Although it would not be the first time she'd sold one of her paintings with the paint yet wet. Violette looked at Assia, curiously, noting that it seemed to be slate-blue that deepened the green in her eyes. Violette smiled—and sighed— aware that the woman's companion had his fingers through the tear in the front of this woman's jeans, which was actually what her smile was for. And her sigh. It had been quite some while since any man had touched her in that sort of way. Public, and personal. A yet deeper sigh wound through. She missed him. *What was Stephen thinking, walking away like that—with not so much as a smallest protest?* She shook her head. Assia raised an eyebrow.

"Assia Greene," Assia said, offering her hand.

"Violette...McEwen." Violette took Assia's hand. Their laughs came at the same time. "You'd be surprised how often it happens—more frequently than one might think—meeting another person with a colour in their name—but there you have it," Violette said. "I once knew a young woman named Indigo Scarlett—such an absolutely entrancing colour-linking— wouldn't you agree?

"I can't quite fathom your seeing the bridge in this painting. I've hardly gotten a start on it. I lived in America—well, one couldn't really say that I lived there—I was in California for several weeks, a few years back, taking care of my son who was in college in there. He was recovering from a surgery, which is why I'd gone over to the States—to California, that is—to help him. The light simply mesmerized me. I'd not seen it before—light, Like This. The sun, so absolutely present. I returned the next fall, to San Francisco. The Golden Gate Bridge compelled me so, and I longed to try painting it. I wasn't able to produce anything close to what I was so captivated with, in looking at it, though I'd started over again and again, in hope. Odd, this—the vantage point, here, by the Thames—synchronicity, perhaps—the light just now over the Houses of Parliament, inspired me. I felt it in me. I could do it, actually, Like This. That is, paint the bridge, finally—the combination of light, intuition, and recall." Violette shook her head. "I'm surprised you see it," she said. "I'm not sure, yet, that I do."

"Ah then, it's true. It is the bridge! I would truly like to purchase the painting. That is, if you're willing to part with it, once finished to your satisfaction. I mean that, sincerely. It's... well, it's antidote—for... for the..." She couldn't name it aloud, to this woman. She could hardly articulate this feeling to Aesop.

"The *abyss*, shall we say? Is that it?" Violette suggested. Assia startled.

Violette looked at Assia's face and nodded. "Yes, I see it. I've heard it said, once, and have never forgotten it either—that 'poetry is the only antidote to regret.' I feel the same about painting. It's my only antidote to despair. I'm extremely grateful for it, I will say that." She turned back toward her painting and with the edge of her paintbrush, caught an errant drip of gold paint as it slipped down the canvas.

Assia leaned backwards into Aesop, his fingers still catching the tear in her jeans. "Violette," she said, "this is my friend, Aesop... Aesop Wind-Rivers." Aesop released his fingers from the threaded-web, and offered his hand to Violette.

"My pleasure," said Violette, blushing at her choice of words. "And what a beautiful name you are graced with, although you must hear that every time you are introduced."

"I have the honor of carrying my great-grandfather's name. Thank you for the compliment. Can't imagine how he came by it—never heard the story. As for the Wind-Rivers part of my name, it's from Wind-Rivers, Wyoming where my ancestors lived. Are you familiar with that part of the United States?"

"No, I'm sorry to say. I've been only to California. I would love to travel more of the Western United States. Can't imagine how, though, come to think of it. Seems I'm tied to all things here, so, with family, work." Violette tipped her head to the side, in thought. Her mind wandered into the sun and the light of Northern California, the way it fell over the sidewalks in San Francisco. Yes, she'd love to be there, yet again. She wondered how her life had become so complicated in these ways, such that she felt that leaving was simply not an option.

"Violette, we don't want to keep you from your work. You must have many interruptions working outside Like This." Assia said. "Please... here's my cell number." She retrieved one of her business cards from the zippered side pocket of her backpack. "Please call when the painting's finished. I'm serious about wanting to purchase it from you."

Assia turned back to Aesop and put her fingers in his belt loops. Standing on tiptoe to whisper in his ear, she nudged him closeandcloser pulling him against her. "Let's go," she said. "We can come back later—if we want..."

Chaucer shifted. Aesop felt a tug on his foot. Chaucer's gold leash had looped around his ankle, the leash pulling tighter as Chaucer *scooched* himself backwards. *Must've happened while tussling with him, earlier*, Aesop thought.

Aesop started to bend down, his intention to loosen the grip of Chaucer's leash, while Assia felt herself yanked forward— sharply, suddenly. She could see that Aesop's belt buckle was caught-up in the loose threads on the front of her jeans, causing the resistance. She leaned back, reflexively. The tear pulled. Aesop's buckle was hopelessly bound in the now-tangled threads, and created a sudden and sizable opening in the worn fabric.

"Aesop!" she said. "Wait a second!" Violette watched the coalescing events, her eyebrow lifted in amusement. *Whatever is going to happen here, it should be interesting, certainly*, she thought. Violette was aware of the slightly shifting newspapers, from the people on the benches behind them. Aesop turned, smiling in spite of the predicament, and began to work the buckle loose from Assia's jeans. "I've gotten into a mess of a maze, I can see that," he said, bound at the waist to Assia, and by the ankle

to Chaucer. Aesop freed the buckle, then squatted down next to Chaucer, coaxing the dog closer to him to allow enough slack in the leash to pull it over his ankle. Violette stepped toward Assia, eyebrows pulled downward as she inspected the now-gaping tear.

"Assia," she said, "Hmmm... I wonder what you might think of this idea. Let me take these for you. I'm a seamstress. I'll stitch them. I can bring them back tomorrow. Right here, this same location. Or, really, whenever would work best for you. I can arrange to be here most any day."

Assia started laughing, the morning's loneliness blessedly forgotten. Aesop looked at Violette, smiling. "You've got to be kidding me," he said. Not that he hadn't heard similar offers. Assia lived in these jeans, and he'd been witness to the threads pulling looser, by the day. Assia shook her head, still laughing. *What does she expect I'm going to do? Take them off, and hand them over?!*

"Take them off, and hand them over, then," Violette said. "You can simply wear... well, let's think about this a moment, shall we? Here it is! You can wear what I have on... Yes! That's it, there's the plan! Here... and for—what is that word?" She tapped her chin. Aesop didn't know when he'd last seen someone tap their chin, in thought. "—*Collateral*, that's it—you can take the painting for now. Try it in your flat. A grand idea, this! We can meet back here tomorrow. If that suits your schedule, that is. I'll be able to repair the trousers—rather, denims—tonight." Aesop's mouth dropped. He hadn't been in England long, but he'd definitely gotten the sense that the British were not as spontaneous—in quite the same manner anyway—as Americans. This incomprehensible offer! He knew immediately that Assia would find an offer such as this one, far too enchanting to pass up.

Assia decided this was exactly what she needed, a ridiculous offer. As if daring herself, she started to pull at the waistband of her jeans, the buttons unbuttoning, giving way, all at once. She thought to glance at the benches along the way, where there were so many of what she referred to as "business types" reading newspapers.

"Okay," she said.

Okay. Violette loved the way Americans so often used the word "okay"—it seemed to fit most anything.

Assia appraised the trade. What was it, exactly, that Violette was wearing? Looked to be a gold and pink skirt, over leggings of deep blue—a sweater that buttoned all the way up the front—high heels. *These British women and their high heels*, Assia thought.

Violette, snugging her belt more tightly to her waist, released the buckle.

Assia, pulling at the laces of her hiking boots, kicked them off, as her jeans slipped past her thighs.

Aesop reached for the paintbrush set on the narrow shelf of the easel; pushing it squarely into the rivuletting gold paint, he touched the brush to the inside of Assia's thigh, winding a slow trail down her now-bare leg—a golden cord, grounding Assia. To herself.

Chaucer stood up.

Assia took in a quick breath.

The skies casting mist turned over itself to a darker shade of pale, and the newspapers shifted. Again. Readying for tomorrow's headlining swoon: OBAMA OBAMA OBAMA... as

Violette turned, and with the tip of her finger caught the drip of gold paint, just as it reached the canvas's edge.

CHAPTER V.

AZURE

Celia was late. Her high heels clicked sharply as she ran up the steps to the Tate. Perhaps Violette had already requested a pot of tea for herself. She so hoped Violette was not too pressed for time to have a look at the painting with her. She opened her purse, reached for her lipstick, pulled the cap from the tube, and swiped it quickly across her lips. Without looking, she replaced the cap, dropping the lipstick into her bag. She walked through the turnstile, nodding to the uniformed guard. *I need to settle myself...* Celia slowed her pace on the smoothly polished tiles; she took in three breaths, deeply, the way her yoga instructor had directed the students to do when they felt a racing sensation in their heart.

Yoga was good for her, she knew that, but the "new age" paradigm did not suit her. She did not want to wear exercise clothes, or the ever-present Birkenstock shoes, which she found rather ridiculous—not meaning to offend anyone with that sentiment. She didn't use a yoga mat, and eventually people stopped commenting on it. She liked the feel of the floor beneath her hands and bare feet. She could identify her *driste*, the point-of-focus, in the lines of the floorboards of the studio, the better to manage balance in *tree pose*, which she fell out of quite regularly, in spite of herself. Or to hold steady in the graced *dancer's pose*.

Celia simply wore whatever she had on, for class, when arriving at the yoga studio, removing one or two bracelets that might be in her way in the yoga poses, the rest of her jewelry left on. Light from the studio windows refracted through the gems on her bracelets as she tipped to triangle pose, *trikonasana*, the *opening of the heart*—the light, coloring the lines over the floor of the studio. She liked the feel of her ankle bracelets slipping, when lifting into *Warrior III*. The delicate-ness of her jewelry grounded her. She didn't want the energy of large muscle movements to take her too far from intricacies.

"My husband—Phillip, that is—is rather adamant that I stop with my yoga," Celia had told her therapist—the one she'd seen when she'd felt hopelessly stuck in her marriage, unable to make any movement with it one way or another. "He refers to it as 'all this yoga,'" she said, raising an eyebrow. "Furthermore, he's irritated with what he calls my 'art-type' endeavors—I suppose he's referring to my writing. Or maybe it's my work at the Tate, agitating him. Who knows? I've given up trying to understand. Exhausting, really.

"What Phillip wants," Celia said, looking at her therapist, drawing her eyebrows inward, "is that I let go of anything to do with myself—anything that's truly about me—and instead, to put my time to 'better use,' as he says. On *his* agenda, that is. He wants me to 'day trade' for him—the stocks and all such as that—while he's at the clinic. Can you imagine? As if! As if I could begin to ferret that out, or have the least interest. Can't think what a mess I'd make of it all, if I were the slightest motivated in that area. Which I'm not. Of course. Do you think Phillip could ever see that? Or see... me?"

Her therapist had put her head in her hands.

Celia wasn't sure what it was exactly, that had caused the stuck-ness she'd felt within herself regarding her marriage, to find a momentum, finally—and a forward one at that—one that took her out of her marriage. She only knew that she felt relief. Not grief. A *stepping into true*, she'd called it. She'd felt herself start to expand into what she'd suppressed of herself during those years, reclaiming "self" from some of the misguided bargains she'd made in the marriage—surprised with the pathways beginning to open.

Celia did not see Violette.

Violette was having a hard time keeping Assia's jeans buttoned. *No zipper—metal buttons—odd.* She'd rolled the cuffs to keep them from getting stuck in the tops of Assia's hiking boots. *Whatever was I thinking? At the very least, I should not have given over the heels. I could've managed the jeans with heels, after all.* Violette shook her head. A total stranger. And yet she trusted she would see Assia the next day, as they'd arranged.

She gave attempt to walking a bit faster, but was dragging in the hiking boots. *I'm probably keeping Celia waiting.* "Come on now, Chaucer-One." She pulled Chaucer along as best she could. *He's probably hungry by now, poor thing.* Violette wasn't sure what to do about that right now. She was not a good dog owner, she knew. Chaucer had been left with her, when Stephen decided to leave. Stephen had left, true. But then it was her doing. She'd told him he could find his own way out and he'd done just that. In retrospect, she realized she'd hoped he would stay. And say something to her. *What? That even though he didn't feel the same feelings, he might? What words would've helped the situation?* There were no words. And only later would she think that it was ironic beyond understanding that the reason she'd left Stephen— all right, asked him to go—wait a minute, *told* him to go—was because she'd fallen in love with him. So different than stepping out of her marriage, which she was fully ready to do—leaving, because the "something" that was supposed to be, was not there at all.

How she'd so quickly married Simon, after Stephen's leaving, was something she could not settle in her mind. She'd wanted the twins to have a man in the house, and Simon was so willing. And available. And she hadn't known what to do with her hurt. Marrying Simon was safe; it had seemed so. Yet, it was wrong—

wrong for her, and wrong to have done that to Simon—never mind that he'd wanted that they marry. What she hadn't known, then, was that missing Stephen would not let go of her after all.

"What the hell are you wearing?" Celia looked at Violette, shaking her head. Violette could be counted on for unusual style; Celia knew that much, clearly. Yet, she'd not had any occasion to have seen clothes of this sort on her friend. Had she seen clothes of this sort at all? That, she doubted. And here was Violette, dressed in impossible-to-overlook ripped jeans. And... *hiking boots?!* Celia was baffled.

"We don't have time for me to tell you the story behind this," said Violette. "Let's take a look at that painting. Hold up a minute, actually... I feel I must have tea first... I'm beyond all reason." Violette often spoke in this way and Celia went along with it. She adored Violette. Violette was beautiful in a way that women loved, and that men didn't understand—most men, that is. Recently, when Celia had been with Violette at a book release event, a man had approached Violette as they were entering the bookstore; he'd simply said, "Are you... an artist? It's refreshing to see someone dressed with the so-unusual style that you're wearing... to put themselves into the world, with such... interest—uniqueness."

He'd backed a couple of steps while making his comments, turned, and walked away, before Violette could think to respond. Celia had watched Violette glance down at her clothing, as if to remind herself what she'd put on that day.

Yet, Celia knew it was more than whatever Violette might wear. It was something else; something Violette seemed to carry about her—a confidence, or rather a "not caring" about others' reactions or responses—a certain sense, noticeable, and yet unable to be quite articulated. Violette dressed for herself—her present mood, or an other need she might have on a given day; she'd wear any combination she felt like, anywhere she went. These jeans, an example—though Celia had to admit they were, yet, much beyond Violette's usual predilections.

As for men's responses to Violette? On more than one occasion, Violette had told Celia there were men who were simply *nonsensically* attracted to her. Men in their corner offices, men who had office security one had to ferret through to stop in to see them, which of course Violette wanted to do—stop in and see them. These men could not make sense of Violette's having circumvented the security, appearing at the threshold of their offices, smiling that smile at them. They'd glance up, distractedly, from their work—quirk an eyebrow at her, and ask, "Just how did you get up here?"

Violette had noted, with her personal mix of confusion and playfulness, "These types of men need to simply not become taken with me. Then I could leave them alone. If I've just come from painting, they agitate about my getting the oils—from my hands, or clothing—on their office furniture. Or on the leather steering wheel of their car, for example. Who knows what-all-fuss they go on and on about," Violette would say.

"Nevertheless," she'd told Celia, "I find it difficult to resist any man who shows an attraction that is of... *a soul's longing.* I suppose that's what it is that's being sensed... a longing that comes from a place within, that they in no way recognize, by the way. It's not productive, of course," she said, "for any true relation. If they don't choose to live there—in those places—that respond to whom I seem to represent for them, what is the good that can come of it? Frustration—that's what comes of it. Yet, I cannot turn away from soul longing. It seems right not to do so. I suppose it is what I am most looking to find. Perhaps that's it."

Assia readjusted the belt, gathering Violette's skirt more tightly around her. "E, what kind of a morning have we had here?" she said, looping her finger through the back of Violette's high heels, pulling them off one-at-a-time, and *scunching* them down into her backpack. Aesop was holding the canvas carefully, hoping not to get wet oil paint on his jacket. In truth, he was not as concerned about any paint on his jacket, worn as it was, but he did not want to smudge the still-wet painting.

"We could get lunch later," Assia suggested. "Perhaps on the train on the way to Cambridge. I'm not hungry yet. Can you wait to eat?" Aesop looked at Assia, writer of his heart and soul and, at present, barefoot writer. He loved Assia. He loved loving her. He thought he'd always loved her, even before they'd met.

"Assia," he said, holding the painting in one hand and pushing Assia's hair from her face with the other, "I think that skirt is not quite right for you. I think it needs to come off. I think a few more things need to come undone before this day has its way with us anymore than it already has. I truly feel disoriented; all the more because that's not a usual state for me—I feel as though I've wandered onstage, smack into the middle of a play, witlessly intersecting a plot I can in no way catch grasp of. All I can say, is that I hope it's non-fiction."

Celia stirred cream into her tea and reached for the sugar.

"I never use sugar at home, yet when in tea shops the whole rhythm of things changes, and it seems sugar is called for— odd, that. . . What is it, love? You seem... in another place. Well, besides the clothing you're wearing, that is."

Violette was sketching her fingers over the peace sign on

the denim of Assia's jeans. She hadn't noticed the detail when Assia was wearing them. Violette lifted the polished copper teapot and poured, warming up Celia's now-lukewarm cup and pouring freshly for herself. "Celia," she sighed, "I have to leave this marriage. I do. I feel so sad for the twins—and Simon, of course. Yet, I need to... I need... to what? What is it I need to do? How should I put it? I need to live more—well... more *honestly*—that's it, I suppose."

Celia looked at Violette over her cup of tea. "Love, I know. It's all right." She paused, waiting to see if Violette needed to say more.

"How is the missing of Stephen going?" Celia asked.

"Dreadfully," said Violette. "This woman I met today—the one whose jeans I'm wearing—can't go into it right now—a story in itself. 'Assia' is the name, I think. The man she was with— 'Aesop'—I've never met anyone with that name. Here, let's have a look at the business card she gave to me. Yes, here it is. Assia Greene. That's right—a colour in her name. Auspicious. She carries a loneliness, Celia. I've been down that deep. All about this woman seemed... incommensurate—I believe that's it— with her ability to hold it; the ache in her pulled at me, nearly *beckoned*. I must say, I'm still trying to ground myself."

"I suppose wearing her clothes is helping with that?" Celia smiled.

Violette was already lost. She remembered the first picture of the Golden Gate Bridge she'd made after returning to England.

Neal had given her some drafting tools: a T-square, French curves, things she'd not known of. She delighted in anchoring the T-square along the edge of her desk, drawing lines against it. Her lines had formed the Golden Gate Bridge before her eyes: Reds. Deep indigos. Lines crisscrossing one another, the rusted-orange of the bridge's ironwork. Saturating light. She could hear horns honking, and could see the sun pouring light on the streets and signs along the boardwalk, illuminating the San Francisco day. The traffic in her drawing was heavier than one would expect for that time of day—the bay a gorgeous azure blue—not typical for the bay, as she recalled it. She'd shown the drawing to Stephen. He was clearly baffled.

"But I thought you were going to show me a picture of the Golden Gate Bridge," he'd said.

"This *is* the Golden Gate Bridge!" And then, "Can't you see the traffic?"

Violette thought it obvious. Stephen stared at it, quizzically.

She'd had no idea what to do about him. Later when they lay on the couch together, the afternoon light stealing over them, she'd tried sorting it out to him, her words hesitant as she searched for just what to say—that falling in love with him had increased her vulnerability beyond her capacity to hold it—and for some reason she thought the right thing to do was—leave. *Why had I thought that? Seemed to have some sort of integrity to it.* That's what she told herself as he let himself out of the flat and she rolled face-forward into the cushions of the couch, and cried.

"I'll slip out of these boots. I can barely manage the jeans as it is. Here, then, I'll put them in my bag. Let's have a look at the painting," Violette said. "After that, I need to attend to major life decisions. Marriage. Divorce. Sewing these jeans."

CHAPTER VI.

INDIGO

That next morning Celia decided she'd take the day away from the Tate; she wanted to see how it felt to structure her own time, in the event that she may yet truly choose to leave her work at the Tate Gallery—its predictable work-day schedule organizing her day for her. *This is the day. Today... I am determined to attend to this November Novel with absolute focus! Or, I will have to abandon it altogether. Four days lagging is as "off-start" as I will allow myself. How many words must I call forth—from the depths, as it will no doubt be—to catch up?*

She'd spread it over the first several days—that was her plan—but at least get a full-on start. Celia put her laptop into her satchel and gave thought to walking to the coffee shop. A day away from navigating London traffic snarls in her MINI, would be a good thing in and of itself. St. James Park was near to a kilometer from her flat. Quite manageable. Perhaps Violette would turn up during the morning. She knew Violette's plan was to return to the spot along the Thames where she'd met the woman and her friend. *The names—what were they? Unusual... started with an "A," both—Hmmm... can't get near to recalling them... I'll ask Violette when I see her.*

Celia wondered if Violette had made progress with the ripped jeans. Violette was a *seamstress extraordinaire*, in Celia's take on it. She was convinced Violette could make a rather decent living with these talents, and had told her so, many a time.

Violette had wanted to leave some of the rips as they were. *That's what she said. I remember that part of the conversation, if not the names of this mystery couple.* Celia didn't ask why the rips were significant enough to let be. It was enough for Celia to trust Violette's intuitive "read" on things, which seemed to follow laws not discernable to the general public. At the very least, her creativity intrigued.

Celia found the coffee shop unusually crowded for an early mid-morning, with laptops about, everywhere she looked. Indeed, November Novel month was popular among the patrons of this particular coffee house. Nate had emailed to Celia that he'd write with her today, supporting her starting this project "at long last," as he'd put it.

Nearly cyclically, one or the other of them—she, or Nate—came to the decision that it would be a rather prudent idea to try to end this "craziness" of being with one another in the ways they were with one another—"craziness" being Nate's term for it—a word choice Celia noted as one of his so "typical Americanisms."

His latest plan for them was that they would write their November Novels together, their contact boundaried by coffee shops, laptops, and word counts, thereby lessening the temptation to touch one another. Together they would, he put it, "wean" her from him. She suggested that he was perhaps having a similar struggle detaching from her, and that the weaning may need to take effect both ways. Yet, she thought hers the likely stronger need. She yearned to lean into the height of him, the substance of him, to help her feel not such the *lone soldier* every single bloody, ding-dang moment of her day-after-days.

What would happen at the end of November? She couldn't simply watch him walk away—drive away. Whatever it was he'd planned, if he had planned at all. Which Celia doubted, mightily. *What was he truly thinking with this latest scheme of his?*

Celia had met Nate when she and Violette were working on the Arthur Hughes exhibit together at the Tate; Nate, having recently arrived in London from San Francisco, had sought out Violette, his sole contact in the city, other than the co-workers he was soon to make acquaintance with. Violette had brought him along that day to show him the Gallery. And Celia didn't care. That he was married, that is. She didn't know she was opening, already, to feelings for him... feelings that fell outside the parameters of "right feelings" for a new friend who turned out to be married. She loved to hear him talk about his young daughters—twins, like Violette's daughters. Good dads attracted Celia. She knew this about herself. It had happened with her before, yet not quite in this way.

At that time, those first several meetings, she wasn't drawn to Nate in any way that was specific, other than as a friend. It happened later, after several meetings, and while she was distracted with complications with the art installation. Yes, she'd been preoccupied, but that hadn't stopped her noticing that she was taken with Nate in a manner not fitting.

She remembers when it happened. They were in a restaurant, the two of them, alone, together—after her colleagues from the installation project had left for another engagement. Celia and Nate had stayed on. Maybe they already knew. His gaze, so intent. She'd never seen eyes that blue, she was sure of that. It was dark in the restaurant. Rain splattered against the awnings and windows. She'd watched the rains steady slip from the awnings edge—distracted. They'd eaten mussels. He must've ordered them. She'd never eaten them before. They had wine. Malbec.

The matter of his marriage... she'd had a *too-long* marriage, which she'd come to think of as a non-marriage. She didn't see marriage in the way she might have had she been at a younger age—her twenties, say. He needed to work out his marriage for himself. It was other things really. It was trying to find that place he talked about when they both admitted they were entangled with one another in ways they could not find the means to sort through—that *comfortable and right place*. Somehow they'd not been able to find it.

The way he'd stood in the entryway to her flat one late afternoon, adjusting his tie, so at ease in that still and personal space, saying something about the meeting he was off to—had all felt so intimate to Celia that it was hard for her not to think of Nate as her husband, married to someone else. She referred to them as "lovers without a context." She couldn't bear to think they were having an affair. *How could I be heart-connected to this man Like This, and struggle so? How could I not?*

That he would leave her, two months into their relationship, close to the time his wife and daughters came over to England, from America, stunned Celia to near shock. She could not get her mind to accept it. Nor her heart. Later, when she could think at all, begin to talk about it—with Violette, of course—she said, "I miss him. Too much, Violette. I miss him with every sense. His hair smelled like... velvet."

Celia looked up when Nate entered the coffee shop, backpack slipping from his shoulder. She was always startled with the pull of attraction she felt for him. Each time. Nate scanned the coffee shop quickly. Eyes landing on Celia, he smiled, and motioned that he was going to order coffee before sitting down. Celia opened her laptop. *I have to start and that is just that.* She tapped her pen on the keyboard absently, letting go all thoughts from the morning, clearing her mind. Nate pulled out the chair across from Celia's, winked at her as he sat down, scattering his backpack and jacket over the chair beside them.

"What happened to your need for caffeine, love?" Celia said.

"What?"

"Your coffee?"

"Oh, they're bringing a pot."

"A whole pot?" Celia shook her head.

"Yeah, that's what they said. Didn't make sense to me, but I figure, whatever—I can drink a pot anyway. I see you've already got your tea going."

"Right... How to begin... Maybe I'll begin with you. Us, that is," Celia said.

"Celie, what are you gonna do—write a soap opera?"

"Nate—I've always loved your calling me 'Celie'... Have I ever told you that? Perhaps not! You're the only person I know to 'nickname' me... It seems a rather American sort of thing to do...

"Hmmm... I should start with a title—is that it?" Celia readjusted her computer screen and clicked through font styles.

"... but then, when I think of it, Nate, my name is a nickname, actually. My parents—musicians, you know—had wanted to name me Cecilia, for Saint Cecilia, the Patron Saint of Music. Did I ever tell you this story? Saint Cecilia was a much-beloved saint, as the tale is told—a beautiful young woman who'd given her life to the service of others. Yet, my father said that he felt a vulnerability he hadn't the damndest notion—that's how he spoke—the damndest notion how to contain, when he first held me, his newborn daughter, in his arms. That it had been then, that he remembered—the name they'd chosen for me was for a saint who'd died too young—and violently so! Since he was the one filling out the birth record, he shortened the name to Celia. As if, Nate. As if a love like that has any say. After all."

Celia swept her eyes up and to the side, quieted. Nate had told her that kind of look—one that he noted her taking on quite often—meant "looking into the future." "Where you come up with notions like that, I haven't a clue," she'd told him.

"Nate, love, help me calculate this, would you? I'm four days late starting this epic—this November Novel. What is that, in word count? What would it be, love? Four, multiplied by 1,667 words—isn't that it? Let me think a bit... must be 'round about 6,000 words, and more."

"Six thousand six hundred sixty-eight, Celie," Nate said, turning in his chair, looking for any sign of coffee headed his way.

"Well, that was an altogether rapid calculation, I'll give you that..."

"Was focused on that goal, myself, just yesterday—stuck in my mind," Nate said. Giving up on coffee for the moment, Nate opened his laptop, tapping his fingers rapid-tempo on the table, impatiently awaiting the few seconds needed for the screen to ready itself to accommodate his energies.

Celia *scunchelled* her body in her chair, and drew in a breath. "All right then... Hmmm... I shall have to get myself sorted through in quick order, won't I?" She absentmidedly tapped her pen on the saucer of her teacup, pondering.

"Here's an idea, Nate. I've given over thought to this idea, before... I'd like to write about *secret griefs*... those types of grief that can't be talked about with anyone—openly, that is. Abortion, for example... carries such secrecy, doesn't it? Shame, rather. I remember never knowing whom I could be open with about my own abortion. Yet, I walked with a grief that quite overtook me; I couldn't look right to left before crossing streets. I was too caught. The added anxiety in having to wonder about bumping smack into judgment...

Or think about this, Nate—affairs. When you're having an affair... Not you, in specific, that is. When *one* is having an affair— and it ends. There's nowhere to go with the grief. It has to be kept secret. The loss of an affair, *extramarital*—is that the word for it? How does one take liberty to feel the feelings, openly? Or to talk with anyone about grief of that sort? Grief needs... air—around it. Needs to be noticed. Held. By others. Certainly by something broader than one's self, alone."

"Celie, sweetheart—November Novel is *fiction*." Nate saw her stricken look. Celia's face could break right before his eyes—shattering-fragile into tiny pieces all at once. He'd seen it happen. Her skin was nearly translucent. There were times he could see the veins and arteries through the surface, giving Celia the air of vulnerability she often evoked. He took pictures of her when she wasn't expecting it, though full well knowing that Celia detested photos of herself. She said she thought of herself "reasonably pretty," until she saw a likeness of herself—and then, as she'd said, she didn't even know why she left her flat. Nate paid no attention to her vanity in this regard, his dilemma being capturing her skin's quality. He'd yet to photograph her skin's luminousness in a way that truly showed what he saw when looking at Celia. Lighting, maybe.

"Wait a minute... I don't mean to hurt your feelings, Celie. What I mean is, that's a great idea. I'm sure it's important, probably—but November Novel is about fiction."

"Oh! Why can't I keep that in my head? I've no idea how to write fiction, really, and that's the truth of it. And, of all things, Nate—I made a bargain with Violette that if she completed, finally, a painting of the Golden Gate Bridge, that I, in turn, would finish these 50,000 words. She got the better side of that arrangement, I see—didn't she, then?"

A young man holding a coffeepot aloft, wandered by, aimlessly.

"Here," Nate said. "Over here. I think that's for me. Have any half-and-half? Sugar? I need plenty of sugar—Celie, I'm listening—justaminute... What's this thing about? This...

coffeepot. Seems to have a cord. What—am I supposed to plug it in and brew my own? Can't figure this out..."

Nate glanced around to see if other tables had coffeepots on them, but he didn't see any.

"You know I never make coffee, Nate. I wouldn't know. Plug it in here where my laptop is, just like an electric teakettle then, love."

"I've no idea how to handle an electric tea kettle," Nate said, bending down, plugging the cord in above Celia's laptop connect. "I'm just going to head over to MacGaffin's and grab a cup 'to go' and come back."

"Nate, hang on, love. Hold a minute... see what happens. How am I to get something done here, with all your figurings out, and your 'this-es' and 'that-es'?"

Violette entered the coffee shop, package under her arm, leather bag over her shoulder. She scanned the wide space, the tables crowded at odd juxtapositions—counters strewn laptop-to-laptop. Her gaze landed on Celia and Nate, and she pulled a nearby chair to their table.

"Ah! I see you have one of those coffeepots! I think yours is actually perking! I couldn't stay long enough while here, yesterday, to see it in motion." Violette slipped her bag and package to the floor. She leaned over, focus intent on the coffeepot—the heating-to-very-hot, coffee-grounds-infused water, erupting over the inside surface of the glass-knobbed top.

"I love to watch this—the coffee—*splurking*, Like This..." Violette said.

"Never know what might catch your interest, Violette," Nate said. "You get caught up with the... oddest, details. Odd to me, anyway. If I could interrupt your reverie... I need a cup of that stuff. I've been waiting too long for caffeine as it is," Nate said.

"Nate, love... it's not ready yet," Violette said.

"What d'you mean... How can you tell?"

"My grandmother had a coffee maker Like This. One needs to watch the coffee, the movement of it, that is... and wait for it to perk to just the right colour—darker than this, love. You'll need to keep an eye on it," she said.

"How about you 'keep an eye on it,' and I write," Nate said. "Could you—for a second, or two? Or whatever the heck it takes? Believe me, I'd be grateful. In fact, if you could catch that first second when the coffee has '*splurked*'—was that your word?—*splurked* itself—into a color that you deem proper for coffee to be *splurked* to, I'd be beyond grateful. I'll dedicate my novel to you. How's that? Speaking of—enough coffee mutiny—need to figure an opening to my next chapter."

"*Chapter*?!" Celia said. "You actually have chapters? Never occurred to me, that. I've not a clue how I'd manage it."

Violeete *scooched* her chair closer to the coffeepot. "The barest split second of 'ready,' and I'll have you happily sipping caffeine—rather, guzzling caffeine, in your case. What is it now, Nate, before you distract into 'November'... How d'you take your coffee, love? I'll have it fully set for you."

"Just pour in a sizable notion of half-and-half," said Celia, not looking up from her computer. "I'll do the sugar. I don't fathom your adding the amount of sugar that Nate takes in his coffee, in all good conscience." She looked up. "Tea, for you, Violette? While you've been put on task? I'm having a warm-up and then I will fall into this novel and not look up." Celia lifted the coppery pot.

"Thank you, I think not. The coffee shouldn't take but a

moment more—a moment too long for this impatient one, though," she said, with a nod toward Nate. "I've only stopped to see if you were here. I'll need to be on my way—to the Thames—hoping to find the couple I met yesterday."

"Yes! Of course! How did the jeans repairing go, then?"

"Very well, actually. I have them here."

"Violette, show the jeans to Nate, will you? Nate, you've a moment to see this, haven't you? Well worth it," Celia said

Nate looked up. "What jeans?"

"I didn't get the full story," Celia said. "I only know that I've never been as surprised with what Violette might be wearing as I was yesterday. And believe me, I'm often surprised with what Violette may have chosen to put together, on any given day." Violette shook out the jeans from the paper wrap that fell away, and onto the floor.

"Hmmm... I've seen many a pair of jeans exactly like that—or shall we say, pretty nearly, exactly like that," Nate said. "Though I can't say I've come across jeans quite this faded and worn, in Britain... definitely American. How'd you come by this extremely well-worn-in pair, Violette? Doesn't seem quite your usual style. D'you mind?" Violette handed them over. Nate put the worn denim of the jeans near his face. *Berkeley...* He could smell it... could smell beer, could see it slopping over rims of glass mugs, soaking the wood flooring. Marijuana. The very scent of it in his mind. The absolute raggedness, strings pulling and trailing at the hems... Everyone he'd known, then, wore ripped-to-tatters jeans, Like This.

"Violette, love, here's an idea." Celia said. "Put them on... Nate can see what I'm talking about."

"Celia! Whatever can you be thinking?! Exchanging clothing in public, once, is one thing—an event that makes me re-think all manner of things, of yesterday—yet again? This will become my mode—I'll want to get dressed in public from here on out."

"I'm serious, love! Try them on... Simply slip them on, under your skirt!"

Violette glanced around the coffee shop. She thought she could manage the theatrics of this sort of move without undue notice. "All right, then," she said. Taking the jeans from Nate while stepping out of her heels, she pulled the jeans on beneath her skirt; she unfastened her skirt, lifting it off over her head. Heads lifted from laptops. These buttons—such a problem for her with these jeans. She gave a yank and a slight jump, to notch them up snugly—and attempted the buttons again.

"Here," Nate said. "I'm more familiar with these than you are." He looped the metal buttons of the jeans into the button holes. Body memory.

"Yes," he said. He leaned back in his chair, studying Violette's newest look. "I see what you mean, Celie—rather non-typical look for you, Violette. The high heels do add an unusual twist. When I think back that far, the last time I wore jeans like that I was barefoot. California lends itself to barefoot. Moreso than Britain," he added.

"I'd best get on my way," Violette said.

She floated her skirt over her head, turning it into place, and pulled the jeans from beneath the skirt. She gave them a quick shake-out, and folded them squarely into the paper packaging.

"Celia... have you a start, yet, on your 'November whatever-it-is'?"

"Trying... I shall definitely need a full-out running start."

"Could I talk to you a moment, then—? That is, before you start?" Violette said, glancing at Nate. "You don't mind, do you, Nate? Nothing to take offense."

"No problem. I'll get some chapters into a head start... new project at work Monday, and I'll have less time for writing than I'd like."

Violette glanced a quick check on the progress of the coffeepot as she and Celia moved to an available table toward the front of the shop. Misting rain whispered wet over the large front window. Rainwater diverted horizontally over the wood divides of the small panes of the window, the glass showing circular designs where actual movement of the glass had occurred over years' and years' time.

"This gloom," Violette said, gazing to the window, "I actually prefer it today... though it may yet challenge my painting outside. Especially if it develops to anything much more than this mist. I assume the couple will keep to the pre-arranged meeting. Should rain deter them, I'm not sure what I'll do, though—how I would contact them. I hadn't considered that when making the arrangements, yesterday. Hmmm... I do have Assia's card, come to think of it. There's the safety, if I'm able to determine where I may have stashed it. There is that...

"I'm running on and on about triviality, Celia—avoiding what I most need to say." Violette took in a breath, her throat catching on the words. "It's... I talked with Simon. This morning. As he was leaving for work. There's no good timing, of course, is there? I finally put words to it, Celia! I told Simon that I 'couldn't be married anymore.' He simply didn't believe me—I could tell that much. Clearly. I don't know what I'm going to do, Celia. It's the right thing. I know it is. Even if no one else can be counted on to bloody well understand it." Violette looked at Celia, eyes bright with tears.

Celia tipped her head to the side, gaze tracing Violette's face.

"I'll be trading one loneliness for another, though, won't I? I see that. It's that this one seems more honest. Honestly, I feel I'm stepping out without a net—that odd way the structure of marriage gives certain illusions. You know."

Celia reached for Violette's hand.

"You see, Celia, that is the very thing Simon could never do. Do you think he could at least hold my hand? Or touch me? Or wait for me, even—so important—when we'd walk up from Picadilly station, for example—the steps, the crowds... rather than walking on ahead? Anything like that...

"And Stephen was worse! The hurt continues on and on. Still! I'm in fixes about the whole mess of it! Stephen, I mean, not Simon. Not as much, anyway.

"I go over it and over it again, in my mind—how things were before I told Stephen I couldn't carry on, with him. Not in that way. How could I—when more than once I 'called the question' about his feelings; he always had the same answer—that, yes, he cared, but 'not as much as you want,' he'd say, or 'not as much as you do.' Honestly, Celia! I get taken with the most insanely ridiculous details in men—the line on Stephen's cheek, or the particular wit he has about the most usual things. Or a look he gives me, certain times, when he doesn't even realize it. Those things bind me to a man with super-gluelike hold."

Violette put her face in her hands.

"I'd thought by putting my energies to other things—my painting, for example—that I'd be protected from caring in the way that is too much—falling damned attracted to someone who's not good for me... Oh! I hate feeling this lost." Her words fell out in a rush.

Celia looked at her friend, reached toward her, tangling her fingers, softly, in the loose wisps of hair curling over Violette's shoulder.

"Violette," she said, "It'll be right, love. All of it will be right. It was the truest thing to do with Simon. You know that... You know that in your heart and soul, love. And Stephen? Well, that can happen to anyone... We get attracted to someone, and then things along the way don't proceed as we'd wanted—the way we think they're going to. Or the way we think they should. Or that we'd hoped.

"So hard, love. I understand that."

Violette nodded.

"I think about my own difficult situation. Nate... What am I to do, in the long run? The medium run, the short run...? The question is, when am I going to do something? He's married, Violette. That's the core of it. When I get myself past the 'what the bloody hell am I doing?', I come to the deeper question, the 'what am I doing to myself?'... a continual struggle. A heart struggle. It's always part, Violette, just part of something.

"Ah, but look, love—I didn't mean to go on about myself. Let's get you your tea before you're out to the weather. Do you feel it necessary to go to the Thames? Might you take the afternoon at home instead? Simon and the twins will be away, won't they? Some time without responsibilities to others around you, would be a relief for you, I believe. Do you want me to come along? I'm just as well frustrated with starting this novel at your place, as here... I'll keep you company, without needing you to do anything. How does that seem?"

Violette nodded. "Yes, yes let's—d'you mind, awfully? Can't think this couple will show. Look at the rain! You could have the sunroom for writing. Ah, but wait! I cleared the furniture from that room. I can't think what's come over me! I'm purging from top-to-bottom. I sold the bookshelves to the woman down the park, for her children. The girls are not yet out of the house and I'm at the ready—clearing it. What will be left by the time I settle myself?" Violette shook her head. "Yes, do let's get tea before we go. Yours will have gone cold by now. We can check Nate's progress, with his *chapters*."

Celia and Violette wound their way back through the tables. "Once he hits stride that's all there is to it—the words pour forth," Celia said, nodding toward Nate.

"Indeed... a laser focus, if I ever saw one," Violette said. She stepped to the counter, ordering more tea for Celia, and a pot for herself. Violette carried a cream pitcher to the table, and moving laptop cords to one side, made a space, at-the-ready.

"Hmmm..." Violette said, giving the coffeepot a look-over. Her eyes followed the length of the cord, to the outlet. "Plugged in, soundly. What holds the grounds and water from circumnavigating correctly?" Finger to the dimple in her chin, Violette pondered the coffeepot quandary.

Celia leaned to push aside an errant piece of hair, flopped over Nate's forehead, as she sat down. "Right, then," she said, "To begin...

PART ONE: *LIKE THIS*

"One of Nate's expressions," she said to Violette. Celia scrolled, brought herself more upright in her chair, and began typing.

"The colour is off-tone," said Violette, looking at the coffeepot. "It's gone pale," she said, "... and to an even lighter shade, rather than darker. Why is that?"

Celia watched letters and words align, hands moving over her keyboard quickly. Nate lifted his hands from his keyboard. Sinking back in his chair, he re-adjusted his vision from the overly-close focus that keyboard work required, looking toward the front window at the rain, eyes scanning around the crowded spaces of the coffee shop. His face clouded. "Okay, there's an example. Right there! Why does that guy have coffee in a regular cup, while I have this infernal coffeepot trying to perk itself into something? Can't understand this..." Nate leaned in his chair. "Excuse me! Where'd you get that coffee?"

A newspaper tucked under one arm, coffee mug held aloft, the man in question looked surprised with Nate's pointed question. "Well, this is a coffee shop, you know," he said.

"Yes, yes, of course," Nate said. "But how did you get coffee, like that—when I have to struggle with brewing my own?"

"Order one," the man said, in bemused confusion. "That's all. I have no idea what you mean, really."

Nate motioned to the coffeepot—perking, now, in alternating light/dark/lighter/and lighter-yet/ brew. "This," he said. He looked around. "I can't understand why I don't see pots on other tables. Or why I have one. I just want some caffeine. I don't want it to be hard."

"Well," said the man, shifting his papers to better balance his mug of coffee, "perhaps you're finding yourself in a different setting than the one I'm in. In the setting I'm in, I can get all the coffee I want—no coffeepots at all." He wandered off toward a table by the window setting his coffee next to his laptop, already opened and humming...

Nate looked dumbfounded. "What the hell is that guy talking about?" he said.

Violette had *scooched* her chair backwards, and was looking under the table. "What happened to the package I had here? Those jeans? I couldn't've put it too far from my backpack. I don't see it, though."

She sat up again, and tapped her chin with her index finger, thinking. Nate was taken with the "chin-tap" that Violette quite often exhibited—clearly it was unconsciously, and for that reason all the more charming. Nate didn't want to call her attention to it, less she self-consciously stop doing it. It *paused* him, in whatever he'd been doing, and *stilled* his thoughts, wherever his mind may have been. If unlucky, one could miss catching it. Nate wondered if it may, in fact, help... if it, indeed, "tapped" something sensical to mind.

Celia bent down to aid her friend in searching under the table for the missing package. Nate scooted his chair back and peered beneath as well. It was the logical spot, hence the double- and triple-checking. In spite of its having last been placed beneath the table, it was nowhere, there, to be found.

"Can't imagine where it would've disappeared to," said Nate. "It was right here. Not that anyone would take it in a place Like This. And no Londoner would pick up a nondescript, brown-paper-wrapped package in a public place; that goes without saying."

Violette sat up, accepting her tea from the server standing, patiently, beside the table. "Ah! Thank you," she said. "D'you mind my asking? I seem to have misplaced a package—wrapped in brown paper. Have you seen it, by chance?"

The server shook his head. He turned back toward the barrister's counter. Grabbing coffee mugs from the hooks over the counter area, he commenced making lattes for the waiting customers. Nate observed—each distinct, minute, choreographed motion. Nate erupted. "This—is making me fucking nuts! I'm going up there and ordering an espresso, like any other person in this coffee shop."

Celia shrugged, a barely suppressed smile playing across her lips. Violette poured the tea, stirring milk into the smoothly scented warmth, thoughts distracted with the missing package.

"Those blue jeans... Do people still call them 'blue jeans?' What could have happened to that package? Ah... I should check on Chaucer. I forget about him, you know. I wonder if I might spot him, from here," Violette said, turning in her chair. "Hmmm... I'd best go out to him. Chaucer will be wondering what's kept me, as it is. I'll be back in a moment, Celia."

Celia started typing. *Anything. Anything to keep this flow in motion, Like This.*

"You got some then! I'm happy for you," Celia said. "Or should I say, two. Is this your version of a 'refill' then?" Celia felt for the edge of Nate's chair under the table, with her foot—and gave it a shove toward him, given that he lacked a free hand to pull his chair out for himself.

"Thanks, sweetheart," Nate said.

"You see? It wasn't so hard, after all, now—was it?" She said, "Your mood will perk in no time." Her eyes returned to her computer screen. "Inadvertent pun," she said, her fingers moving words over the page.

"I had to get somebody else to order it for me," Nate said, moving the coffeepot to the floor and pushing his laptop a few inches forward, clearing more space to set his espressos. He scrolled backwards through his on-screen pages, scanning for the last left-off paragraph. "I'm not even gonna to try to understand it," he said, eyes on the flashing screen.

Celia raised an eyebrow.

"Okay, no kidding, Celie—" Nate looked up. "I couldn't get

the barista-guy to take my order for coffee. He started handing me a different kind of coffeepot. I lost it. 'I already have a frickin' pot!' I told him. 'All I want is coffee. A cup. Coffee. That's all I want.' There was a guy walking nearer to me. If I'd realized he wasn't heading up to order coffee, I might not have bothered him. I asked him if he'd mind just getting an espresso for me... told him I'd pay for his, as well. Little did he know how much I'd pay. Turns out he'd just stopped in to grab a *New York Times*, and was headed right back out. That's when I decided to 'go for it' and ask him to order two—figured it might be my one chance. He said, 'No problem.' That's it. He stepped right up and ordered both espressos for me, no questions asked. I thought about trying to offer some kind of explanation—as if I could—but when he handed me the espressos, he said, 'Don't worry about it.'"

"Hmmm..." Celia said, looking at her screen. "I'm lucky to have only tea to manage. More well-behaved. So much more dependable."

Nate stared at the words on his laptop, and began to type in earnest.

"I've managed who-knows-how-many words, of who-knows-what; I've thousands, yet, to catch up to. I can't believe I've not given it to lost cause! As yet, that is... "

"Here's a thought, love," said Celia. "I could look for a character carrying a secret grief—the kind I was talking about. An affair, for example... I didn't mean us, Nate—you and I, that is. I never see it that way—us—an affair... though, I'm not the one married." *That might've been... pointed*, she thought. More than once, Celia had wanted to ask Nate if he thought of himself as having an affair with her. *Why wouldn't I simply ask?*

"Celie, I've got an idea... might help you with some word count, get you further into your start. I could have my character—I have simply one character, you know—I could have him intersect one of yours, in your novel... the same interlude in each of our novels. They could meet briefly—our characters—'ships passing in the night,' that whole thing. In a restaurant maybe... or a bar... You could change it to a pub, rather, if your setting is England. They could bump into one another—I mean, literally, and introduce themselves to one another, and then, who knows what, after that. What d'you think? Who've you got?"

"A moment, Nate... Let me look about in these words. I've a near beginning as it is. A few characters floating in-and-about—all rather vaguely to this point... not awfully much going. Hold up... hmmm... Here's one, actually... a male character. I'll see what his storyline is. There's a chance he may be carrying the grief I'd hoped to write about. Not that I'd wish grief on anyone, mind you. It's just that it would be so convenient for my idea."

"Understood," said Nate.

Celia was absorbed, focused intently on observing the emergent character in her barely beginning novel. "Wait! It's taking form. Indeed. Ah... deep grief. And yes! Secret! Perfectly serendipitous, that...

"Oh!" Celia sighed, concerned. "Such a heavy-on-his-heart *sorrow*. I'm *so* sorry! Not sure what it is... Wait! It's—it's about... a... a woman...

"Well, that's rather cliché, isn't it?" Celia shrugged. "Can't be helped. Seems something tragic happened to her—rather sudden... *What was it?* Her name is—*Mystery*—the woman he's grieving."

Nate looked up from his keyboard. "*Mystery...*" he repeated.

"Yes, that's her name," Celia said.

"Celie, how can someone's name be— *Mystery*? Well, of

course—I know, in theory at least, a name can be most anything, but…"

"I don't know, love—that's just her name—I had nothing to do with it; it's the name she arrived with.

"Nate. . . what? You're giving me that 'look.' Look, love—if I'm to write fiction, the only way for it, is to simply… well, to open myself—like a channel, I suppose… to let the words come through—from where, I can't begin to know." She looked up at him, brows drawn down in earnestness.

"I can't *make up* fiction, Nate. You understand that, surely."

Nate paused.

"I lack imagination, Nate. That's the long-and-the-short of it."

"Celie, anyone walking in to your apartment—'flat,'—would know at first look, that imagination is not anything you lack."

"What? D'you mean the… furniture? Is that what you're thinking…that the couch, the chairs, and the bookcases are placed at all unusual angles into the room, away from the walls? It's about the light… how it falls across the walls and floors in lines and angles. You've seen it, Nate—you've photographed it, in fact. Light from the east windows throws itself across the walls in the mornings. If I keep things out of the way, I can give the light its due space; I can watch the light move. Or… the colours… is that it? The turquoise blue of the ceiling? I love that colour… perfect, for the ceiling. Experimentation, Nate… Others lack the time, I suppose. Or the inclination. Perhaps that's it.

"That's not imagination, Nate. It's… *logic*. That's all it is, love. Rather obvious, isn't it?"

Celia's description of *light* cued Nate—not to the room in Celia's flat where the light from the east windows fell across the room; it was her face he saw—here, across from him—light, breezing spirit over her lashes, and cheeks.

Have I ever really looked at Celie? Have I looked at her enough?

Celia's focus returned to her computer screen. "Hang on... Clarity speaks, yet. My story... the character, the one who's grieving so—for this woman, Mystery—seems he's entering a place. He's unaccompanied. Solo. Looks like a crowded sort of spot. I s'pose it could be a pub. No, it's not a pub, actually— too lively. And much bigger than a pub. It's evening... or rather, night—that's it. Late. I'll type this setting to the screen while it's showing itself in such detail."

Nate was drawing Celia's face with his eyes, and his mind— fusing it to memory—her brow, the curve of her cheek, the lift of gold hair caught in her right-side earring.

"Right, then... are you ready for me?"

Tears, unexpected, tripped his words. "I could never be ready for you, Ms. Celia Brennan-Garrick. That's a compliment, by the way," he said.

"All right. How 'bout this," Nate said. "My character will bump into yours, in this crowd... it's crowded. Did I make that part up, or did I get that right? My character will ask your character his name—and I can only imagine what that might turn out to be—then my character will go on his way. Something easy like that... won't give you too many words, but might jump- start something. Tell me his response, and I'll write it into my novel."

"Well, hey... what's your name?" *Nate was taken aback. He looked around. Not sure about that overly friendly bar patron... was this a gay bar, or mixed?*

"Nate's the name," he said, almost relieved that the music may have drowned out his voice.

"Nate? Nate's your name... really! Well that's..."

"He's not responding... much," Celia said, eyes on the words jumping across her screen... seems sort of taken aback. But then, of course... what would I expect? He says his name to your character—Oh! So sorry, Nate! I missed it!—his name. Altogether too noisy in that place... whatever kind of place it was."

Nate paused, again—thought to say something. Couldn't think what.

Precipitation splattered the windows in a rush. "I'm worried about Violette. Where is she?" Celia said.

Violette unhooked Chaucer's leash from the bicycle rack that was next to the front of the coffee shop. *Used to be tea shops everywhere. Now, coffee shops. Why is that?* She didn't know. Though she preferred tea, she liked coffee well enough. Celia wouldn't go near it.

"Chaucer, what d'you think—could we chance taking you inside? It would give me a better eye on you..." *Doubtful*, she thought.

"Let's position you under this awning a touch further—it'll keep you drier on the chance these clouds decide not to hold. I'll gather my things. You and I can be on our way. And where that will be, Chaucer, my friend, it's yet hard to predict."

Violette was never sure how to talk to Chaucer—her default was to simply talk to him as she would a person. She'd no experience with dogs—or animals of any kind, until Stephen brought Chaucer home one evening. Even then, it was such a short time between Chaucer's arrival and Stephen's leaving that she was without experience enough to pattern herself after. The twins liked Chaucer fine, but they were more than busy with their senior projects and university applications, with little time for much of anything else.

What will next year be like, with the girls away? Violette leaned her back into the bike rack, momentarily lost in thought. *Jessamine's applying to Cambridge, for literature, makes perfect sense. Francesca's interests... hard to say with that child... wide ranging, is most likely the best way to put it. The University of Edinburgh is probably a right choice for her.* With the girls' academics, she thought it likely for each to gain admittance to the university of their choice. *Cambridge will be a bit of a challenge, regarding admittance,* Violette thought, *but Jessamine could pull it off if anyone could.*

Violette was relieved that Francesca would graduate at all. Francesca had nearly left school that horrific year when migraines leveled her with a vengeance. *Eli.* Worry had shell-shocked the family, settling a dark fury in Francesca with migraine headaches that would not abate. Hospitalized through days and nights, Francesca was worn ragged with the intractable pain. Violette had felt one thing, and only one: *Helpless.*

She stood near. That was all she knew to do—to be *the one who accompanied*, the one holding vigil—while doctors and nurses pushed narcotics into her young daughter's veins, searching among farther reaches for the key that would turn the trajectory.

Violette smiled at Chaucer, his brown eyes beseeching. She wove her fingers through the silkiness of him and secured his leash. Violette glanced skyward again. The rain seemed emergent, adamantly so. Violette scooted Chaucer further under the awning for protection should the clouds unleash while she was inside to get her things. Entering the coffee shop, she saw Nate sprinting on his laptop.

What was it... two cups of coffee on the table beside his computer?—the coffeepot nowhere to be seen. Celia was also, finally, working—from the looks of it. Violette didn't want to disturb either of them. *I'll manage on my own*, Violette thought. *Celia can come by later.*

Violette despaired leaving without knowing what had happened to the jeans. *What can I possibly tell this engaging woman, Assia?* Violette tapped her chin... thought. *Can't imagine. I remember taking them off, folding them. Then what? Hadn't I put them back in the paper?*

The young man working at the table under the front window closed his laptop, and tipped back in his chair. He pulled back into a stretch, and exhaled a deep sigh at the precise moment that Chaucer, in a motion too sudden to catch a warning glimpse of, leapt into the windowpane with a *thunk* that shook the nearby tables. Violette instinctively spun toward the window. "Chaucer!"

Violette stepped quickly toward the door—turning back, briefly, as she passed the table where the young man was set up with his work. "I'm so sorry," Violette said, "That's my dog... I've no idea what's got into him. Did he startle you? Must have..."

"A bit. Yes. It's fine, really—looks as though he's settling again," he said, looking through the front window where he could see the dog, gold leash tangled through the bike rack. Violette peered through the window. Chaucer was *scooching* into the wall, under the awning. "Perhaps something startled the fellow," the man said. He looked at Violette, quizzically. "Are you the one looking for the brown paper package, by chance?"

"Yes! You've seen it?! How did you know?"

"It's here, on the chair at my table. I was going to bring it to you, but I saw that those two were both rather focused. I thought I'd wait for a break in their work concentration, and then take it over—people don't like to be interrupted when they're hard at work like that... and I planned to be here awhile anyway. I've no idea how the package came to be at this table. It was here when I sat down. Have to say, I had that panic, first noticing it—y'know, that initial momentary paranoia we're all supposed to have about packages."

"I shouldn't have wrapped it that way," Violette said. "Why didn't I simply put it in my bag?" She shook her head, relieved beyond any confusion she might share with him, that the package had turned up on the chair next to his table.

"Thank you! Ever so much! You've no idea. It's not even mine. It was my plan to return the contents to the rightful owner, today."

"What is it? That is, if I may ask."

Violette peered out the window to reassure herself of Chaucer's status.

"Of course—it's a pair of jeans that I was mending for someone. A favorite pair. Of hers, I mean. Or should I say, it seemed quite so, from what I observed. Therefore, a prized possession in that regard, if not inherently valuable."

"I see... although, all the same..." he said, "if I may be so bold as to say so—jeans should never be mended. They're better, the more worn and frayed."

Violette looked at him. "Actually, I've never worn jeans. Well, other than the particular pair in question. Yesterday, in fact... but that's another story." Violette noted the laptop on his table. "Do tell me... you're working on the November Novel—correct?"

"November Novel... never heard of it. What is it? Sounds like an entity unto itself, the way you say it."

"You're asking the wrong person, I'm afraid. I don't understand it, myself, other than that my friend and her... her..." Violette trailed off. She typically stumbled over how to refer to Nate. Especially since he wore a wedding ring, and given his obvious affection toward Celia, most observers would assume that he and Celia were married. Yet, they weren't. Not together, anyway. Therefore, "husband" was clearly off. "Boyfriend" didn't seem fitting... "her *friend*—are writing it. They must, for some odd reason that, again, I couldn't explain to you—churn out somewhere near to seventeen-hundred words, per day, each day of the month—November. I'm not much of a writer myself; I prefer painting, sewing—As it is, I hardly like computers."

The man retrieved the package from the seat of the chair—obscured beneath the tabletop—and held it out to Violette. As she reached for it, Violette's brows drew downward in confusion. "Ah," she sighed. "That's not it... How very, very disappointing."

Chaucer suddenly, again, leapt at the window, this time hitting the glass with such force that the small panes of the coffee shop window looked as though they would give way. Every head turned. Violette screamed.

"Chaucer!"

He hit it again. Glass cracked wildly splintering skittering sparks crashing splattering chairs tabletops laptops Celia jumped chairs rocketed tables in singular choreographed motion every person on cue stood, covering ears Nate at the door Violette stepping through Chaucer glass ricocheting scattering shards over plates coffee mugs tea pots cups but that was nothing. Nothing at all compared to the explosion.

CHAPTER VII.

SCARLET

Assia's characters were giving her a run for her money this morning. She was worried. She had no desire to write an adventure novel. She didn't want to write into anything that she'd lack knowing how to contain—yet, her characters seemed at sea—in a storm that she hadn't been able to write them away from.

That wasn't at all the setting they'd been in when she'd last logged off. *How did they get there?* She sensed *danger. Of what? Washing overboard?*

The foreboding warning unsettled Assia. She sat back in her chair, staring at the screen from a distance, as if for protection.

I don't think I want to face this...

I most certainly can't afford to lose even one of these characters—especially now—they've bound with one another.

She took in an anxious breath. She had no idea how she'd fallen into this story that was writing itself.

I need to get outside. I've been too long in this flat without talking to another person—besides these characters having an explosion of dialog this morning—so very active, and distracted, and looking for something... What was it? They'd been intently looking...

Assia grabbed her rain jacket; pulling one sleeve over her arm, she bent over her computer to tap the log-off key pattern. *Now what's happening?* she thought. *Something that will not be put off.* Assia sighed. She stood over her computer, rain jacket trailing off one shoulder, intending to tap this out quickly—whatever it was—

I'll just get these words, she thought, *and then head out to intercept Aesop at the Thames—can't imagine Violette would be there in this rain... good that I didn't try to send the painting with Aesop today.*

What's this? Assia was alarmed. Her characters had been thrown from one another suddenly—at once. Chaos wrote itself across the screen. Assia stared in disbelief... *They're in a disaster of some kind. What kind though?!*

Whatever it was, it had hit with a force Assia didn't have words for. She scanned wildly for her characters—worried most especially about one, in particular—a character with a storyline gaining a complexity that Assia had wanted to pursue. Not that she had much say in this novel of hers. If any.

Aesop notched the collar of his jacket, wanting for a hood for better coverage in the rain. Assia planned to meet him at the Thames, if making enough progress toward her word count this morning. Aesop was trying to be supportive of this mission of hers—this November Novel—though he didn't know quite how to do that. The writing had been getting tough for her, the latter part of this first week. She'd said the second week was reported to be a challenging juncture, when getting in the near-to two thousand words for the day became noticeably more difficult. She feared leaning too much on Aesop with this project of hers, and hoped to find a blog to log onto for support.

Assia had said that her characters simply stepped into the story—or were there already, somewhere—maybe sitting at a table, or on the other end of a phone call, awaiting her notice, their names and storylines mid-stream. She simply logged-in and tried to keep up with them. There were two or three of the characters she'd been feeling a growing attachment to, with the requisite vulnerability in having no idea what might happen to them in the course of the writing.

So like Assia, Aesop thought. Writing, especially a sprint like November Novel, was not his venue of interest. He liked writing, and was often engaged in that endeavor as a lawyer. Not fiction, though. Usually not.

Aesop picked up his pace in the increasingly blowing rain. The wail of emergency vehicles resounded as the Thames came to view... the distinctively haunting British siren call: *beee booo beee booo*. Eerie, mingled as it was with the pounding precipitation that Aesop thought highly unusual for England for this time of year.

Rain hit hard on the benches along the walkways, its staccato-like force propelling raindrops higher and higher. Aesop's eyes trailed police cars trailing fire trucks. Emergency vehicles were not out of keeping for London, although the growing number of them surprised him. He didn't expect the painter woman, Violette, to meet them here given the rain; yet, on the off chance she'd come, he did not want her kept waiting in the downpour. The rain was not about to relent. He'd need to get under cover.

Another ambulance hit speed, rounding the corner in front of Aesop, hurtling the streets collected rainwater up and over the curb in a rush. Ambulance siren lights glanced shadowed blood-red reflections off the streetlamps along the Thames—flickering, in the increasingly dense overcast. *Wonder what this is about?* Aesop thought.

The explosion threw Nate aloft, unconsciousness muting his abrasioning, skin-to-pavement skid across the narrow street in front of the coffee shop.

Violette, disentangling Chaucer's leash, was knocked violently sideways. She stumblingly tried to regather balance, as the iron railing of the bike rack rose up to meet her cheekbone, smacking into it as she fell. Time slowed, drifted. Violette floated. She saw it—the paintbrush hovering, suspended, just... *there*. She grabbed hold of it, willing her fingers' grasp. A florescent green viscosity dripped from the paintbrush—*adrenaline*—and began painting over the inside of her skin, beginning at her left wrist, moving up her arm, turning... winding... and painting, painting.

Someone was *breathing her,* with deep inhales that opened her lungs, fusing mind to consciousness. Vision was slow. She felt her way to clenching ever more tightly to Chaucer's leash. Pulling against the bike rack amidst unraveling brain tangles, she propelled her body upwards. Unsteady, her mind was unable to right itself in tandem with her upright position. She could not reach for Chaucer to pick him up in her arms, a picture running incessantly and repetitively, looping her brain. She lacked accessing her mind's willingness to engage in physical motion. She could pull on the leash at half-strength, only, until the adrenaline wound down her arms and into her hands and she yanked Chaucer's leash with renewed strength—pulling him, dragging him, toward the other side of the street.

The other side of the street was not far enough.

Debris rained, pummeling the sidewalk, pounding imprinting thuds in Violette's brain. Violette reflexively covered her head with one hand, Chaucer's leash tightly around the other; she inched Chaucer further away, past the street she had finally, finally, crossed, with him. The slow-motion maze would not be sped forward, no matter her efforts.

The coffee shop imploded recklessly, violently, in jarring discord. Disbelief. Violette's hearing silenced. Her vision slid into narrow, and narrower, yet—until the entirety of what she could see in her mind's eye was nothing at all, save for a thin gold line—shining, connecting her to Chaucer.

Nate sifted through layers of semi-consciousness. He felt himself reach... *It* was one finger-tip past his grasp. Layer-after-murky-layer morphed to translucent, then foggy, again. Lifting, sinking, in blurred semi-consciousness, Nate was mired in mind-fog. Powerlessness. Scared him senseless. He tried to speak. Nothing. He tried again. And again. Nothing. Each time, nothing.

Nate felt the sensation of being lifted. He couldn't make sense of it. He heard someone saying his name—over, and over. He answered. Over, and over. At least he thought he was answering, but he couldn't satisfy whomever it was calling his name. A too-bright light shown in his eyes, he couldn't do anything about that, either. Celia came toward him—again, and again. Yet, not close enough. *A fingertip's distance.* She was saying words, holding her hand to him. He reached for her, again. *I have to leave now, Nate. I love you. You know that,* she said.

He tried to say it—*Where are you going?* But there were no words. Darkness.

Enough! Assia said, shoving her chair away from the desk. She glanced toward the windows where rain pelted chaotically. *Can't think that I've seen rain quite Like This intensity for some time,* she thought. *Certainly not in England.*

Rain or not, Assia decided she had to have a break from being in the flat, working solo Like This. She needed to take in longer-distanced vision to counterbalance the too-close visual range that was eye-to-computer-screen. Her brain needed settling. Assia felt franticness that was too close to her. Not taking time to find her umbrella, she grabbed the key from the hook by the door and yanked the door open, stepping onto the landing. Pulling the heavy door behind her, she jammed the key in the lock, turned it quickly, and jumped down the steps, rainwater splashing up around her legs. One sleeve on, and one yet off, she hit the sidewalk running. *It fell... Blue light fell from her pocket in the morning when she ran in the rain...*

Assia stepped under an awning along the street's storefronts to escape the rainstorm's lashing. She'd called Aesop on his cell, but he wasn't picking up; she realized she wouldn't be able to hear him at all in the rain's fury.

What was I thinking, heading out in this weather? I'll have to hope for a taxi. She started walking in the direction of the Thames, thinking she might yet catch Aesop, in spite of the rain, but as Assia rounded the corner onto St. James, she was abruptly stopped. Yellow police tape cordoned the entire area. There was no way to enter.

Warning signals blinked, adamantly, scattering ominous orange hues over emergency vehicles parked at odd angles up and down the street. On the tops of squad cars, sirens flashed, spinning—throwing red light wildly arcing. . . Radios squawked. The rain fell, incessantly. Unrelenting...

"What the hell happened?!"

She felt goose bumps skimming her arms and legs. A crowd had gathered near the taped-off area.

"... big explosion... haven't heard anything about it, yet."

Glass and hunks of plaster fell over the area where the coffee shop had been. Unwieldy sections of the small-paned front window heaped, crumpled, on the street. The building was leveled. Ambulances waited. Though Assia could see that anyone unlucky enough to have been in the coffee shop that morning could not have survived the fall of mortar, plaster, glass, wood. She couldn't imagine it.

Rescue responders carried a body from the wreckage and,

even from this distance, Assia could see that the face was covered with a cloth. Assia felt sick. To think she'd sat there yesterday, with Aesop, at the table in the front window, trying to get her novel started these days behind schedule.

She could not take it in. She could not turn away.

Violette sat along the curb of a side street, sobbing, her face pressed to Chaucer's back. She knew she needed to get Chaucer to a vet. She knew she should get herself checked by a medic. She was in pain. A lump had formed on the side of her head; she could feel that her cheek was swollen, but she couldn't bear to touch her head or face, to assess the injuries. Chaucer was wet with blood running scarlet—matted, in the rain. She wasn't sure where the blood was coming from.

Nate! Her consciousness had begun to clear, in long, slow, undulating waves that washed images inward, along with fears. He'd been close behind her, exiting the coffee shop just as the explosion hit. Before Violette could leap to worry for Nate, the next wave was upon her, this one bringing Celia's face to her mind's eye. Violette's thoughts sped frantically through mind-mazes, attempting any detour for the horrific realization—Celia had not come out with them. Violette panicked. *Anything! Anything... Something! I need something. Think! I need to think!* Anything to assuage her rapidly rising hysteria. *Celia. Celia!* She'd been at the table... Violette had been beside herself to get to Chaucer. *What about Celia? Had she gotten out? Did everyone get out? Did some? Any?* She'd heard the explosion as she was reaching for Chaucer's leash. *No one could have had warning. Could they?*

What the hell had happened? Where was Celia?
She had to go back...

Anarchy.

Emergency vehicles could not move. People rushed forward, beneath or through the yellow police tapes, toward the still-falling wreckage. *How could that be? How could objects be falling, and... falling, continuously, from the sky?*

Pieces of walls, tin ceiling squares, glass windowpanes, electronics, coffee machines—coffeepots, cords flying—china, pottery, pages upon pages of pale blue paper, rain-sogged, drafting. Oddest thing—*what was it?... looked like...* rose petals... And—*What else?* Stardust! Glittering sparks, ashes, and flickering lights. Colours raining down like gold dust—dark greens, deep purple. All of it unimaginable in exploding debris.

It fell.

It would not stop.

Like the rain.

Smells permeated: dust, debris, and blood, and the smell of damp and wet, and—roses. All, in the soaking rain.

Families and loved ones had somehow heard the news and had arrived, frenzied. Unable to wait for responders and rescuers they were beside themselves to get to the growing heap of debris, to use their own hands. To lift. To search.

They made things worse.

They got in the way.

They became hysterical.

They got hurt.

They would not be re-directed.

The police had vastly underestimated what would be needed for crowd control. *The coffee shop was not that big,* Assia thought. *How could there be so many frantic people?* More police arrived, but could not get through the crowd. Violette was blocked. She could not get close enough to the wreckage to even begin to look for Celia. She saw the heap of debris piling before her and felt faint.

Assia saw Violette, first, before seeing the dog's leash tightened around Violette's wrist—Assia's eye followed the leash's length, to the dog. The dog appeared to be injured, with blood dripping through its light-coloured fur, soaked from the rain. Assia pulled her jacket hood more tightly around her face and put her hand above her eyes to keep the rain from them, hoping to hold Violette in view. She couldn't figure a way to get to Violette and the dog. She could see Violette starting to sway, slipping to the ground, her hand still wound through the dog's leash.

Where the hell was Aesop? He often kept his cell phone off, which panicked Assia at a time Like This. Not that she'd, before, had a time Like This. She scanned for possibilities—thought she'd lose sight of Violette if she went around the perimeter of the scene to circle back to her. She had no idea what to do. It looked as though no one did—everything, surrealistically frozen.

There was no still point. Everything was in motion. Helicopters hovered, floating in suspended animation in the drifting-down debris, the propellers rapid chopping muffled in the wild wet. Assia was not sure what could be done to create order in this scene. Wreckage *thunked*. Rain pounded.

Her cell phone vibrated. *Aesop.* Aesop talked to Assia the entire time it took him to traverse the remaining kilometers to St. James Park—shouting, in hopes that she might hear him above the storm. Assia could not hear a word.

Assia had lost sight of Violette and the dog. Scared, she trailed the area, trying to circle back to the place she'd last seen Violette.

Aesop was speechless when he finally grabbed Assia in his arms and looked over her head toward the aftermath. Though, he couldn't really call it an "aftermath." Unidentifiable objects tumbled down... and down, through the skies overcast, settling, clanking and breaking, in the rain's wild downpour. It didn't make sense to him. He'd heard there had been an explosion, but he couldn't imagine the force of it. Drifting particles continually resettled—blowing, shifting, floating...

Helplessness.

Where to begin.

How to stop.

Who are they all looking for?

He knew the November Novel phenomenon had started to crowd the shop, as it had been the day he and Assia were there. Every table filled. Each day. But he couldn't recall how filled it may have been when he'd stopped in this morning to pick up a *New York Times* on his way to work. He held off the panicky thought—how close had he come to wrong timing?

The day Celia's ID'd computer bag was recovered from the *minefield of disaster*—Violette's term for it—Nate woke up. Violette wasn't there. She wasn't at either place—the recovery area, or the hospital. She was on the train to Edinburgh with Francesca, to the University for admissions testing. Simon had called to let her know.

Nate had awakened only to hear news that would sink him to despair worse than his unconscious state. This is what he'd awakened for? To hear that Celia was one unaccounted for and presumed dead, in the explosion?

Nate could only say, "Oh my God"... and "No"... words that became the entirety of his post-unconsciousness vocabulary.

His last memory was *sitting across from Celie. She'd just gotten a start on her November Novel; he'd seen she was really cranking out the words. That gal could type faster than anyone he knew. He could see she'd gotten some sort of run, started... characters... plot. Something, anyway. She'd be caught up in a few days' time at that rate. He had no memory of the explosion. No memory of the sound, the falling debris...*

He'd had the espressos next to him. Violette had gone out to check on Chaucer. Wait a minute... Violette was talking to that guy at the table under the front windows, near the door. Here it is... Chaucer kept jumping at the window, hard. Then glass broke into the shop all over the place.

That was as far as his thoughts sifted before Celia's face came to his conscious mind and he lost all words.

Violette functioned in shock in a way she would not be able to understand when, for moments only, she emerged into the light of day.

How am I doing this?... getting dressed, placing one foot in front of the other, parenting these so-active daughters?

Especially since she'd told Simon to leave as soon as she'd gotten back from St. James Park that very afternoon.

Violette had tripped up the front steps of their brownstone, pulling a bleeding Chaucer along beside her—Simon, alarmed to speechlessness. *Thank God* he was home early. Unusually so. His last client of the day lived near, and he'd come directly home rather than return to the offices. Violette needed seeing to: a bump had risen on the front of her head; swelling, red and tender-looking, extending through the mid-line of her forehead and over her left cheek. Chaucer was a mess. Simon could see that right away. How they'd weathered finding their way home was something he'd never figure. Simon did all he could to hold himself in check, to triage the situation. He'd called an ambulance, but Violette insisted they take the auto.

He thought she'd lost all sanity. He didn't believe her when she said she wanted him to leave. As if he'd leave her, Like This. Yet, Violette was adamant, with a mounting hysteria he couldn't calm. The more hysterical she became, the more convinced he was that he needed to stay. He would have called a friend to stay with her, but he could only think of Celia. And that of course was the problem... Celia.

It was at the hospital, while Simon was looking through Violette's bag for her Health ID card, that he came upon Assia's business card. *Not unlike Violette to collect a business card, or two*, he thought, *when painting in public settings.*

ASSIA GREENE, WRITER

"Writer"... Violette did tend to attract "artist types," he thought.

He recalled the card a few days later, when deciding that he had to take a chance. He needed more help with this... "situation," than he'd at first thought. Violette's parents were in Australia. He'd initially told them he didn't think it necessary for them to come. Perhaps someone else, anyone, in the meantime. He'd figured this would be rough for Violette... plenty rough. But Simon had had no idea.

Assia put her elbows on the surface of her desk, head in hands. She closed her eyes. *This is too much,* she thought. *This November Novel...* Truthfully, she felt ill-equipped to see her characters through the aftermath of something Like This. She found herself trying to hold off a creeping-in, ominous sense; she couldn't figure out what had happened to one of her characters, the one she'd been unable to find—female—someone writing the November Novel. She opened her eyes and scrolled backwards, forwards—scanning words, staring at the computer screen for a long moment, as if willing it.

It kept raining and raining in her novel. She didn't know what to do about that, either. She still had 1224 words to go for the day's word count. *How can I manage it?* Besides that, she'd deleted an entire section, in spite of the directive that in November Novel one is not supposed to make changes.

Her characters were not lining up right; she'd forgotten that one of them was married, with children—she'd made a huge error in the plot-line for that character. She knew that some people writing November Novel had outlines, and lists of characters—but she had none of these. She'd simply logged-on, and the novel already seemed to have its own pace. She felt, most often, that she was along for the ride, and that this particular ride was set at high speed.

Time did not move. At all. Not that Violette could determine. She looked at the clock and it was always the same. Not a minute later. *How am I doing this—walking through these hours, these days?* The twins, of course, needed so much. She had to sign this-and-that application, and form, for testing, and who knows what-all. She could manage that—signing her name. She could manage to check in at work. And sometimes she could even manage to take part in the art therapy sessions she'd been contracted for, at the London Community Center. What she could not do was eat. Or sleep. Or paint. Or call anyone. Even Nate.

Your vows you've broken, like my heart. / Oh, why did you so enrapture me? / Now I remain a world apart. / But my heart remains in captivity. / ... Greensleeves was all my joy. / Greensleeves was my delight. / Greensleeves was my heart of gold... (Greensleeves)

CHAPTER VIII.

TURQUOISE

The memorial service for Celia was on the eleventh of November, eleven days before the Feast Day of St. Cecilia. Nate was still in hospital. Violette had hoped he'd be able to attend the service, for his sake as well as hers. She'd wanted to sit next to him, to lean her shoulder into his—an image from the soothing lines of Rumi that she'd copied onto a piece of pale blue paper, folded, and put in the pocket of her jacket:

Are you looking for me? / I am in the next seat. / My shoulder is against yours.

What could Nate have said, if anything at all, at the memorial service for Celia? What context would anyone have had for him, in Celia's life? Could he have spoken of his love for her? Could he have said, *All I wanted, was to be with Celie, and find that place— that comfortable and right place. Celie was... my heart of gold.*

Silence fell deeply through the breath of early afternoon, on the day of Celia's memorial service. Gold leaves scattered sidewalks and alleyways adjacent the chapel, the air bright— pure as conception. Vehicles were parked tightly against curbs along the cobbled streets. Sun spun spirit-light over the steps leading to the ancient door of the chapel. Violette placed her fingertips into the deeply etched green leaves in the glass panels of the thick door. She trailed her hands along the half-inch tiles of bright turquoise mosaics running edge-to-edge, not missing a beat where curving into the arch of the ceiling. Even the adjacent storage room, collecting cast-off boxes and set-aside antique fixtures, was graced with tiled mosaic ceilings. Brass doors polished beyond innocence opened to narrow, side-by-side closets. *What was stored, within?*

The crowd filled the chapel, spilling through the doors,

onto the steps and into the street. Celia's family sat in the front row, Violette with them.

Blue light fell... It fell through parallel shafts of light streaming through stained glass windows; it fell over the sacred space where Celia's father sat in *stillness*, his bow poised, artfully, over the strings of the cello. His head tipped to the side, he looked up, hearing the music before beginning to play. *Mystery*—the higher harmonic of ethereal knowing. He nodded. And began, drawing the hauntingly lyrical *Greensleeves* from the strings. Tears slipped. Unspoken words tangled heartbreak. Violette, sitting next to Celia's brother, pressed her face into the sleeve of his jacket to stop her tears, holding tight to the grief she would not let go.

Are you looking for me?/ I am in the next seat. / My shoulder is against yours. / You will not find me in the stupas, / not in Indian shrine rooms, / nor in synagogues, / not in cathedrals, not in masses, nor kirtans... / When you really look for me, you will see me / instantly/ You will find me in the tiniest house of time.

— Rumi

The day the turquoise-beaded bracelet was sifted from the debris, Nate was released from the hospital. His wife and twin daughters had come to bring him home. They'd been steady visitors, of course. And, of course, Nate could say nothing about Celia.

Violette had identified the bracelet as Celia's; the one Celia had worn every day, on her left ankle. Violette took possession of it. She couldn't bear to wear it. Nate couldn't think of looking at it.

The investigation was yet in process. Only one body had been recovered; with forty-four unaccounted for. No one had claimed responsibility. Nate had no idea if the explosion was related to the package, the one Violette had thought would be the jeans she'd brought into the coffee shop that morning, but that had turned out not to be. He'd seen the man hold a package toward Violette, and saw Violette shaking her head, signifying that it was not the one she was looking for. *The guy seemed normal enough—how would I know?... didn't seem noticeable in any specific way that might link him to someone who'd be packing a bomb, for God's sake. Whatever type that would be.*

Damn it, Celie... What was it she'd last been talking about, that idea of hers—the "secret grief" thing? Thoughts came frustratingly slowly to him. The doctors and therapists had told Nate that his recall would improve exponentially—in the same way that young children acquire language skills—but that in his case, until the swelling abated, it would take time... waiting. Not something that Nate had ever thought himself very skilled with—"waiting"...

There are certain griefs that we need to process in secret, not in the open, because... Why? She'd given an example. Abortion, that was it. He hadn't known her then. At least, not that he could recall, at this point. Who knows what he knew when? *And what was the other example—that other secret grief she'd talked about?*

She'd been so upset when he'd reminded her that November Novel was fiction. *So like Celia to think she could only write non-*

fiction. He'd seen her completely hit stride that morning, all of a sudden.

Nate returned home to a marriage he did not recognize.

And Nate did everything he could to avoid thinking of Celia.

And Nate did everything he could to recall each detail, of Celia.

It was, yet, November—Nate had half an idea that he could resume his November Novel. He'd saved it to his home computer. *This would be... what?—six days behind?* What else could he do? He couldn't return to work yet. He wondered if it might help him pick up lost threads of himself, to return to something he'd been writing before the accident. He hadn't been able to face his email, nor his computer either, until today.

Nate logged on—224 emails. *How could that be?* The usual miasma of emails... and then, people concerned, he supposed. *Okay... later, on those.* He scanned through the list for anything that seemed of imminent import, and that's when he saw it— Celia's email address, the date of the explosion right next to it.

Nate sat back. He shook his head, slowly. He didn't think he could open it. *She must've emailed that morning.* Nate settled in his chair, scooted it back further yet—reached forward from that distance, and clicked on Celia's email. The time. They would've been in the coffee shop at that time.

An attachment. A note.

Nate took a deep breath, agitatedly pushing the hair from his forehead—*Can I face this? No. Absolutely... completely... not. Can't do it.* After a long moment, Nate opened the email.

Nate—here you sit with your two cups of espresso

typing away at full speed, on one of your CHAPTERS, no doubt—think I've gotten a start, finally, on this November Novel. A bit of one, anyway... the beginning: Part One: "Like This" // Will attach the excerpt. Nate, love, don't be mad, please, when you read it... (No one will ever see it.) I said I wouldn't write about us. And I tried not to. Guess I can't seem to write fiction, after all, just as I thought. Changed a few things—I didn't say we met at the Tate... I'm having us meet on a ferry. I thought that was romantic. So, here it is. See the attached.

ILY, C.

Nate clicked on the attachment, impatiently waiting the interminable few seconds for the attachment to unfold down the length of his computer screen.

PART I: "LIKE THIS"

Later, when they'd started meeting one another, it was always this restaurant. He wanted to sit at the tables outside. Always. In the rain, even, or the cold. San Francisco-boy-turned-City-of-London man. The outdoor tables where it was dark, save the valiant tiny strung-up lights... green, violet, turquoise, gold...

But there were times when they'd find themselves inside, at a small table, so tippy that his coffee would slip up and over the rim soaking the napkins...

She liked to sit in the corner spots, so she could scootch close-and-closer, shecouldnotgethimcloseenough. She wondered, now and then... Did he? What would happen, here? His gold wedding ring catching the light, those so-blue eyes continually, constantly, turning back to hers, Like This. Red wine, still as prayer. His cell phone continually blinking, blinking, like the foghorns and lights on the water, that night of the ferry—blinking: on :: off :: on :: off :: on ::

They ordered mussels. And Malbec. Once, their favorite waitress, Penelope Skye (that could not possibly be her "real" name, they always said), brought a book to their table that explained where mussels come from, when they'd asked her—"Do they find their shells or make their shells—these mussels?"

He would ask for figs again, which he'd had the very first time they were there, when they'd sat by the window next to the street. Rain ran ribbons down the windowpane while she'd tried, so hard, not to fall in love with him.

The hardest part, always, was his letting her go when it was time for him to leave her flat at night. He could never, of course, come to bed with her and stay the night.

"What would you do with me?" He always wanted to know.

Why would he ask that?

"I'd hold your hand all night long," she said. "I'd put my cheek on top of yours."

He knew that piece of her—the leave-taking—how hard it was for her. So he left, slowly. She called it his "leaving-slow"—he'd stand up and wander, talking to her. . . Then, he'd sit down, again. "I have a few minutes," he'd say.

And when close to the door, he'd always turn and hug her, hard, with a force that would push her backwards into the coat closet they were standing in front of, making her laugh.

Once, when it seemed the leaving was more abrupt, he'd called her from his cell phone, having barely started down the narrow street by her flat.

He knew these things about her. She wondered if it touched him. And just how. He would always turn at the front iron gate to look back at her, and she would stand on the step, for a minute or more, after he'd left. She didn't know quite why, even.

Simon called Assia Greene.
Aesop booked a flight for Washington D.C.
Assia logged on to November Novel.
Violette walked up the steps to her brownstone.
Nate wept.

CHAPTER IX.

ANGELS SIGHING BLUE

Aesop grabbed his jacket from the coat hook in the outer offices. He'd put in enough of a day as a barrister. Funny, that word. *Lawyer* was odd enough. And who would've thought he'd come to study law? Perhaps his great-grandfather Aesop. Maybe...

Assia had planned to meet him at a Thai restaurant off Islington High Street. Aesop was somewhat worried about Assia. Then again, when had he not been somewhat worried about Assia? He knew that each day might bring an email from her saying that she'd "had it"—that she was *done* with November Novel. Spent... She'd no more words. Or the opposite—that the novel was writing itself, and she couldn't keep up. Now and again, she emailed an excerpt to him that was so out of any context he may, lately, have been appraised of, that he had little idea what it referred to. Yet, Assia's writing carried a poetry within, that caught him up, context or not. *As did she.* Assia answered something for him that he hadn't realized he'd been asking, until he met her.

Aesop hoped she'd be ready to return to America with him in two weeks' time; he'd lately taken notice of her growing attachment to London. Assia had been homesick as recently as a week past, yet Aesop could see her emergent involvement with life in London. She'd insisted on two apartments for their time here, in London, rather than sharing a place together—a preference that had surprised Aesop given Assia's so often missing his being with her. She'd been concerned that her erratic writing schedule would be disruptive for him, and that the tiny, more studio-like flats lacked space enough for her to both set up a place for writing, and allow living space, enough, for the two of them.

Assia was already seated when Aesop walked in.

As I expected, Aesop thought, glimpsing the gold of Violette's skirt floating over the side of Assia's chair. He'd become accustomed to it—Assia's wearing the skirt that Violette had offered her in the exchange with the jeans. Aesop understood the unlikelihood of Assia's finding a ready replacement for those particular jeans, yet the frequency with which she wore Violette's skirt baffled him.

"Aesop!" Assia typically greeted Aesop exuberantly, as if it were a great good fortune, delightful coincidence, or had been a long time since she'd laid eyes on him. Aesop was charmed with her enthusiasm.

"Aesop," she said, "weirdest thing... a man called me today... said he was Violette's husband, y'know, the painter, Violette. My jeans—all of that... E., here, take this one," Assia said, "I've already looked at the menu. He's been very concerned about her—Violette, I mean—since that horrific explosion. D'you recall I'd seen her at the scene... wandering? And then looking as though she may have passed out—and that I couldn't get to her? Her husband—Simon's the name—found my card in her purse... wondered if I knew her well—couldn't imagine that I did, or why Violette had my card. But he's rather desperate, which is why he called." The waiter waited, patiently, as Assia spoke to Aesop.

"Assia—sweetheart, let's get our order in. I'll have my usual. What have you decided, Assh?" The waiter departed with their orders, returning shortly with the requested water.

"Simon wanted to know if I could see her—Violette. Of course, I'm happy to do anything I can. Why wouldn't I? Anyone would.

"I told him that I'd only just met her the day before the accident. He said that Violette lost her longtime very closest friend, in the... explosion. Can you imagine, E? So, so sad. I told him I'd be glad to help. But, Aesop, I have to say the thought did come to me, that this is finally my link back to her. Right out of the blue. I had no idea how to find her again, since she hasn't been back to the spot along the Thames where we'd met with her that first time. Or certainly not the times we've made it a point to check back.

"I'm struck with her loss. I am! In no way would I want to risk seeming the least selfish. Yet, it's true, Aesop, that at least—at last—I could get my jeans back!

"Oh! That does sound petty and selfish. What am I thinking?" she said, shaking her head.

The waiter arranged their food on the table. On afterthought, Aesop ordered wine—Malbec, if they had it—the only wine Assia liked.

Managing grief's intensity—privately, and secretly, in the midst of family life—all, while as yet unable to return to the distractions of work, immobilized Nate. He'd begun to wonder about the advisability of a change in venue altogether. *What?* Or *where?* The only thing that came readily to mind, as possibility, was San Francisco—the city he'd lived in and loved, for so many years. San Francisco would be quite a trip to make. He missed that city—the deep blue of the San Francisco Bay, the morning fog, the warmth and sun of lazy early afternoons. He missed his close friends—Neal, especially.

Nate hadn't had any expectation that the transfer from California to the London offices would take on the "ongoing" look that it had. Without Celia, he felt detached from London. Grief, of course—that was the largest part of it, the *ennui*—he knew that. He hadn't realized just how much his having felt connected and comfortable in this city had been entwined with Celia.

San Francisco: A week. Two, maybe... Perhaps more. Perhaps

he could reclaim some strength, physically—and emotionally. At the least, he'd have greater openness to *feel* his grief, for Celia. To have, and to hold it. To find, somehow, a way to let it through. Could he hold *her*, if he let go his grief? Such were his mind-scape wanderings.

He'd talk with Lauren about it—leaving London, for a while, on his own. She wouldn't like the idea—the "single parenting," his being away. Nevertheless, he knew he needed to find *that place*, to save himself. *If I yet can*, he thought. He needed to get himself somewhere—geographically, and emotionally—so that that kind of wondering stopped. He needed to not wonder if he could yet re-ground himself. He needed to start. In whatever way he could think to try. Tomorrow was not soon enough. He'd book a flight.

Violette took Chaucer for a walk, something she did not routinely do, now, given that she was not outside to paint, nor to the coffee shop to check in on Celia and Nate and their writing. She tried to get herself to work each day for at least a couple of hours. Contracting her work time independently allowed more flexibility than her psyche knew how to handle right now.

Francesca and Jessamine had made plans for the long winter break that was to begin the next week. Their travels would take them to Australia for two weeks, to stay with Violette's parents. For the other two weeks, they'd travel with school friends. An expensive venture, but Violette had supported it. Had to. She needed time. To herself.

Celia hovered. In her mind, and heart. Nearly every minute. That, in uneasy coexistence with the loss of her relationship with Stephen, and the adjustments to living separately from Simon. At least the one—Simon's leaving the house—felt right to her, timing notwithstanding. She'd had half a thought to let Simon stay in the house, thinking she could move to Celia's flat. Whenever the thought came to mind, she knew she couldn't face Celia's flat and manage her grief.

Stephen had called when he'd heard about Celia. Violette's connecting with Stephen provided solace for her. She hadn't found it helpful to stop seeing Stephen altogether. She missed him, very much, and found it nearly impossible not to email to him each day—going so far as to finally suggest to Stephen that he block her name from his email inbox—that she couldn't seem to let go on her own. He'd replied that he didn't see the need to do that, and he didn't want to. Violette was greatly relieved.

Oh!—to have tea with Celia, and talk about this, talk about anything at all, talk about everything. Celia had struggled so much with her relationship with Nate much of last year, and had finally seemed to be in a comfortable place with it. Violette hadn't thought to pay more attention to Celia's struggles of late... *Regret. Harder than grief. Sometimes.* What was it she used to say? About poetry being the only antidote...? It made her think of painting, but she couldn't think to lose herself in painting. Not yet. The daylight hours were depressively short in November. *Narrow.* She typically spiraled into the lost-ness, in November.

She knew she should get to Celia's flat and help pack things. She couldn't begin to imagine it. Celia's family was far away, mired in this grief that was too heavy for them. They'd returned to Ireland just after the memorial service, unable to bring themselves to enter Celia's flat. Celia's father playing the cello at Celia's memorial service had completely undone Violette. She was sure the deep, smooth notes, issued forth in the *agony of the unspeakable* had fused to her flesh, bones, and soul in a way that would shadow her. Always.

Did *she* want any of Celia's things? Items of clothing—? Jewelry? *Ah! All too hard.* Celia had an eye for colour and style that sparked wonder, and ideas. Celia had had a sense for detail that Violette loved. Violette had often referred to Celia as an artist, though Celia hadn't seen that in herself.

Violette thought she'd have to let go. All of it. Celia's possessions, that is; that she'd be too unable to have Celia's things around her bringing the too-close-to-her-grief closer still.

Assia tried Violette's number again. Simon had given her the number that she clicked into her cell phone over and over. Her fourth attempt. She left yet another message:

"Violette!... It's Assia—Assia Greene. Violette, I'm so... I'm just so sorry—for your loss. Your husband—or rather separated spouse—sorry, I don't know how to phrase that—gave me your number. I have your clothes... the one's we'd exchanged... and your painting, of course. I'd be very interested in seeing you—not for the clothes!—rather, to see how I can support you during this horrific time. Again, I'm so sorry. So, so sorry. I know this is an impossible time, for you. If you can, please call."

Violette thought. She supposed it wouldn't hurt to ring her. She knew Assia would most likely keep trying. *Maybe there's something here*, she thought. *Maybe Assia would be willing to come to Celia's flat, to meet me there. Assia hadn't known Celia; she might not find it too hard to help pack Celia's things, and decide what to do with them.*

Nate arrived in San Francisco at late afternoon's turnover to earliest evening, sun's light reaching horizontally over the Bay, as if to hold itself in place and not truly set after all. After checking in at his hotel, Nate decided to walk to the Pier.

Violette set up her easel. She looked out at the long line of the Thames. Chaucer, skittish of late, was unable to manage sitting as he used to while Violette painted—but then Violette was agitated as well. She pulled paint tubes from her backpack and lined them along the sidewalk, next to her easel. The array of paints would spark something for her. That's what she hoped. She needed inspiration. She needed something. Anything. Anything other than this hollowed emptiness.

Nate stepped onto the ferry. He'd rarely been on a ferry, and yet, since arriving in San Francisco, he'd bought a ticket each day. His routine was set—after boarding the ferry, he'd find a spot along the railing and fix his vision on a point as far out as he could, into the nowhere. *Or was it "the everywhere?"*... losing himself in the Bay's blue. His way back to "found"—that's what he hoped. The each-day-on-the-ferry was obsession—an odd one, for Nate, given that he didn't particularly like water— either the being in it, or on it. His attraction to the Bay area had surprised him, way back then. Though it was true that he loved much about it—the fog in the early morning that lay like a secret over the city—the architecture of the Golden Gate Bridge, its lines and angles; geometrics—triangles, trapezoids, diamonds... Diamonds that breezed a warm magic, sparkling the Bay's blue in the lifting fog.

Nate knew sunlight was antidote to his grief; it was right that he'd returned to California—a right thing, too, that he'd added an extension to his leave from work and made the all-of-a-sudden decision to come here. Lauren didn't understand, but then how could he have expected her to?

Focusing through the viewfinder of his Minolta, finger on

the shutter release, Nate snapped the last rays of late-afternoon sun glinting off San Francisco Bay. In England, these mid-November early evenings brought a duskiness that Celia called *the angst hours*. The light's too soon leaving the day discouraged her, she'd said. She felt as though she were *waning*, along with the light. She preferred bright daylight, or darkness—either, preferable to "the angst hours." A preference that always struck Neal as not fitting Celia's more nuanced sensibilities.

Celie would've loved California. Why hadn't I gotten her over here to see this light? Not that we could have traveled together— perhaps we could've figured something... business trip. Anything.

Nate drew in his breath deeply, exhaling in a sigh. He sighed a lot, lately. *Loss.* He was glad he'd seen Violette before leaving for the U.S. He knew they were each trying to avoid the deepest part of their grief by staying separate from one another. Yet, he'd lately come to feel that their separateness had brought an intensifying of their loss of Celia, instead.

What is it about seeing Violette that is both hard and helpful at the same time? Nate wondered. He saw much of Celia in Violette. The two had been friends since childhood. They shared mannerisms—the way each lifted an eyebrow when something struck them as oddly funny... a certain tilt of the head when in deep thought.

When he'd finally broken the silence in calling Violette, she sounded relieved to hear from him. When she heard he was taking time away, taking off for San Francisco, she'd made a request of him—one that he'd do his best to honor. She'd asked if he'd take pictures of the Golden Gate Bridge for her. Violette thought she might try to paint again—specifically, to keep good on her promise to Celia to finish a painting of the Golden Gate

Bridge. She'd told Nate that she could affix the colours with no trouble, yet had been unable to paint the lighting.

Nate had taken hundreds of photos of the Golden Gate Bridge in past years. He'd download them, later—see if anything might be suitable for her, for whatever he could figure Violette might be looking for, which he knew was something only Violette would know. She'd know it, when she saw it. For Celia's best friend, he'd try.

Nate took pictures each day, uploading an assorted range of them and sending them to Violette, each night, just before he went to bed for those restless, unable-to-sleep hours... Nate adjusted the lens on his camera. Today's late-afternoon light was unusual—enough so, that it might be what she needed. Maybe this—the sun lifting its last yellow-gold graced notes from the ironwork geometrics of the bridge, Like This... Maybe this would be right.

Maybe nothing would be right.

It was true—Violette hoped to start work on the Golden Gate bridge painting, again—yet, she lacked the inspired energy she'd depended upon: the *focused-into-distracted* artistic energies.

Lately, Nate had taken to sending rafts of photos that had nothing to do with the bridge. Urban scenes. Atypical... This latest—a young child, running, while putting on her so-palest pink jacket, with one sleeve on, and one, yet off. *How had he thought, and so quickly, to capture it?*... A woman ascending a curving stairway, light from a high-up side window illuminating the faraway look in her eyes. *What was she seeing?*... The trolley, from the position of the tracks... Grace Cathedral at night—its labyrinth winding circular paths in front of the cathedral—stars falling like *mystery*.

She missed California. She missed being near enough to the Golden Gate Bridge to see its rusted colours... There were the odd moments when Violette had a thought of moving there. Family and work tied her to this part of the world. Yet...

Violette startled as Chaucer leapt up, pulling at his leash. She'd thought to secure the leash by wrapping it around one of the easel supports—which now, had caught, counter-ballast to Chaucer's leash—and Chaucer. Post the explosion, any suddenness in Chaucer's movements set off an instantaneous anxious response in Violette.

"Chaucer! What is it, love?" Chaucer pulled more tightly against the leash, tipping the easel. Violette let go her paintbrush; she caught the easel with one hand, while untangling the leash with the other. Chaucer was insistent, agitating—whatever it was that had drawn the intensity of his focus would not be easily distracted from.

The last thing Violette wanted was to have to chase after Chaucer. It was busy along the Thames—crowded. She despaired at the thought of Chaucer's personal havoc spilling over the walkways. "Chaucer! What's caught you so? Show me!" Violette picked up her pace as the leash yanked tightly in her hands. Chaucer, always captivated with wheels in motion was in quick pursuit of a teenage boy on a skateboard. The lad slowed, enthused to see Chaucer bounding up to him.

"Ah! *Bon jour!*" He bent down to Chaucer, scratching him vigorously behind the ears while Chaucer jumped into him in what looked to be full-on bliss. The boy glanced up at Violette.

He reached a hand to her, keeping a wriggling Chaucer happy by tussling him with his other hand:

"*Jean-Oscar. Enchante.*"

"Violette... *Bon Jour, avec plaisir,*" she said, shaking his hand.

Violette, delighted with his name and his polite expressiveness, was yet more captivated with his obvious and instantaneous affection for Chaucer. The enthusiasm looked mutual, as though Chaucer and the boy recognized one another. *And oh, for Celia*, who spoke fluent French—and with a beautiful accent, as well. Violette had struggled with her second-term French. In her experience, language was never a barrier for communicating with people who approached her when she painted outside. She'd had many "conversations" along the Thames, while painting—with people who had no English, and she no words in their native Somali, Spanish, Hindi, or the many languages that confluenced in London.

Jean-Oscar knelt eye-level with Chaucer, patting him vigorously. Chaucer needed it, Violette could see that. Jean-Oscar talked to Chaucer in rapid, excited French. Violette tipped her head, looking at them. She tapped her chin, thinking. Inspiration. *Could this be what I most need right now?*

Simon moved his things from the London home that he and Violette had shared.

Nate stepped onto the ferry at San Francisco Bay.

Assia wrote her 1700 words for the day in *November Novel*.

Aesop did not know what to do about returning to America.

Violette hired the boy on the skateboard to take care of Chaucer, for what would be an indeterminate period of time, and booked a flight to California.

Violette thought about the synchronicity in finding Jean-Oscar... in Chaucer's finding Jean-Oscar, more accurately. Jean-Oscar was too good a find for Violette to let go. She'd exchanged phones numbers with him, hers scrawled on the back of a deposit slip that she took from her checkbook. She did not have a business card to give him. Simon had always been "after her" to have business cards available for those who stopped to look at her paintings, yet, a sense of business acumen was not Violette's forte. She painted, regardless, not for a business—although she had thought, and more than once, that what she would most like is to make her living with her soul's passion—painting.

Jean-Oscar's name fascinated Violette. She'd always loved names unusual to her. She liked knowing their origins, yet she'd accepted Chaucer's name as matter of course. In and of itself, an unusual name, for a dog... more so, for a person, in this day and age, certainly. She knew "Chaucer" was the author of *Canterbury Tales*, not that she'd read it. She could call Stephen and ask how he'd chosen that name, if indeed he was the one who had—but then, she was trying to keep from contacting Stephen. It set her up for disappointment, and too much hurt, in the longer run of it.

Oh, that man! Finally, she'd met a man who was not ostensibly unavailable to her—married, for example... or gay. Although, how could she possibly have any regrets regarding Neal. She couldn't.

He appeared to like her so much—Stephen did. She'd been

completely open with Stephen, telling him that her heart was breaking in a relationship that was "not to be," and that she wasn't in a position to date anyone. He'd persisted, even though knowing that her heart was yet entangled with Neal. She'd leaned on Celia, much, through the beginning of that relationship.

Violette had been closed to any feelings for Stephen. She accompanied him to dinner, finally, simply because she needed distraction from her frustrated longings. Returning to England from California had not given her the heart distance she'd needed from Neal. To her surprise, she'd found herself missing California as well.

For quite some time, Violette was not open to Stephen. And then, one afternoon, when Stephen absentmindedly reached for her hand while puzzling over an abstract sculpture at an art opening she'd dragged him to, she realized he'd opened her grieving heart to light, and hope.

No one was more surprised than she. Her feelings shifted. To her amazement, she found herself falling for Stephen ever more deeply. His became the name she listened for on phone messages, his the name she scanned her emails for. She missed him when they weren't together. She was developing attachments to certain specific things about him—the soft wool blanket on his bed, deep navy in colour, that she loved to feel against her skin... the couch in the living area of his garret flat, with the worn leather cushions that she would fall into when her days had been all too much for her.

He was forever sending her out the door, saying: "I need to get ready for my classes—and I'm sure you have a full day ahead of you." She didn't get many words from him. His being the "scientist" and, thereby, less word oriented than she, Violette tried to give him some understanding on the verbal interactions.

Still, she longed for him to say, "I missed you," or "I'm so happy you're here." Even once. Or, "Stay"—that's what she wanted him to say, most of all: *Stay*. But he never did.

She'd had a hard time not touching Stephen—tracing the perfect straightness of his nose, tapping the dimple in his chin with her fingertip. She'd cover every square inch of his body with her hands. His touch was uniquely sweet. And sure. It brought her to *still*. But later, when she'd sit next to him on the leather couch, and he'd have one arm draped over the armrest and the other propped behind his head, she felt alone, with him. One of those arms, at least, could have been around her. She longed for the simplest touch from him.

The last time they'd been together was especially frustrating for Violette... Stephen had gotten out of the car ahead of her and was halfway to the door of the restaurant, all the while not even noticing that she'd been held back to wait for a taxi that was pulling away from the curb, in her path. She saw Stephen reach his hand behind him, and for a moment she'd felt charmed, thinking that he was reaching back for her hand. But instead, he was holding his key-fob back, and behind himself, pointed in the direction of his Fiat, to lock it. She heard the locks click shut.

During dinner, his eyes had looked over her head to the television mounted high on the wall behind her. When driving home, there had been too much pause in the conversation. He'd said she could come up to his flat to see what he'd been working on... Once there, Violette felt sad in having forgotten so many things about his flat. It had been too long. When he drove to her home, she was barely out of his Fiat before he'd started down the street, away from her. He was long out of sight before she'd reached her door. She felt safe enough—that wasn't it. It was this: she felt unaccompanied, undesired.

After their breakup, which had been very soon after that so frustrating evening, she'd missed Stephen... with an ache that left her in tears, at night, when she got ready for bed. She wanted to find a way to stop yearning. She wanted to let go.

Aesop was curious, wondering how things had gone with the two, Assia and Violette. He knew that Assia's heart went out to anyone with a difficult loss, even if she didn't know them well. He also knew that Assia hoped to get her jeans back safely in her possession, mended or not. Assia had taken the painting with her, to meet Violette, thinking the unfinished painting might encourage Violette to paint again. Simon had reported that Violette hadn't painted since the accident.

Assia sighed, adjusting her armload of items—the unfinished painting, and a bouquet of yellow jonquils wrapped in newsprint, purchased at a small flower stand near the Underground. Tucked into the side zip pocket of her jacket, she had a beautiful necklace for Violette, found a few days previous, in a tiny shop that seemed to appear out of nowhere... a necklace of mysteriously translucent green beads on a brushed-gold chain.

In Assia's experience with the attendant loneliness of deep grief, she'd found that wearing something beautiful and ascribing meaning to it, could provide comfort. She hoped it might represent something connective for Violette—a symbol of her love for Celia, her friend, a belief in art and beauty again. If none of those things, the simple gesture from one soul to another in a time of grievous loss.

Assia had gone without women friends for too long. She wasn't sure why. She longed for peers, for *kind*. She was all the more sorry Violette had lost her friend.

Nate checked the time. He thought he'd stop in at the office that was linked to his home office in London. He knew if he didn't engage himself in work to some degree, that he'd wander ever more aimlessly in despair.

He missed his daughters and called them every day. He knew it was important that he not be gone too long, for their sakes. But he needed a place to think about Celia. She'd been so right about that "secret grief" theory of hers. How could he grieve her openly? How could he grieve inside his marriage and family, for someone they didn't know, and would have too many questions about? Questions he wouldn't know how to answer.

Violette had given Assia an address in a part of the city Assia was vaguely familiar with, and could find via the underground. She usually preferred riding the red buses, which allowed her to visually orient her location from the windows. But she was in a bit of a hurry. She'd found it challenging, though, to navigate the transfers in underground stops with all her packages.

Violette paced. She walked up and down the front steps leading to a door—the entryway to the stairway up to Celia's flat—once daring to peek through the large rectangular beveled glass door window, noting within the darkened interior the row of mail slots. She was what people referred to as "morbidly curious." She didn't know whether she'd actually be able to walk up that stairway, or step across the threshold into Celia's flat. Assia's meeting her here would ground her anxiety—her silent plea.

Aesop, the last one in the offices for the day, locked the door and walked down the massive front steps of the law building, managing to catch a cab right away. He was too tired to deal with the buses or the underground this evening. He merely wanted to get home, see Assia, and hear how things had gone. He was more and more concerned that Assia would delay their trip back to America, and while he could probably stay on longer at the London office—take on another project, likely—he most wanted to be back in D.C. He wondered if it was time that he and Assia moved in together, there—in that city they both loved. He knew she didn't want to marry again. But he knew he wanted her with him.

Assia saw Violette on the steps and would've waved a greeting had her hands not been full.

"Violette!" Assia called. She hoped Violette would come down the steps and take the bouquet of flowers, at least. But Violette's eyes were unseeing.

"Thank you Assia—for coming." Violette stood without moving, nor offering a hand. Assia set her packages on the step, stepped forward and hugged Violette, feeling the awkwardness in Violette's faint response.

"I'm so, so sorry for the loss of your friend, Celia! I can't imagine what you're going through. I'll try to help in whatever way I can." Tears sprang to Assia's eyes. She scrutinized Violette's blank stare.

"Is this your flat then, Violette?"

"No. No, actually I live a bit of a jaunt off St. James Park. This is Celia's flat."

"Really? I'd assumed this address I was given was your home. Have you been back here at all, since the a—the accident?"

"No. Couldn't. I'd thought you could help me with this, given that you didn't know her—Celia—and wouldn't be as affected in seeing her things and being in her flat. I haven't been here since a few days before the... the... Odd that I can never think what to call it. Doubtful that anyone's been here. Can't imagine who else would come, actually." Violette fingered the key in her hand, and looked toward the door, not moving.

"Do you want me to open it?" said Assia. "It's no problem. You can stand back a bit. Take all the time you need. I'll go in first." She took the key, gently, from Violette's tightened fingers. Assia stepped to the door. *What am I doing?* she thought. She unlocked the beveled glass door, finding herself in the front foyer of the building, numbered mail slots lining the wall to her left.

"Number four, up two sets of stairs," Violette said. "It's the smaller key, for the door to Celia's flat."

Violette stayed behind on the step, thinking. She was not going to be able go in, after all, now that she was this close. Tears crowded her throat, stuck. She didn't know if she'd cried, since Celia's death. She exhaled. *Despondency.* She watched Assia push open the inner entryway door, and disappear around the curve of the stairway and up to Celia's flat.

Assia called back over her shoulder, "Whatever you want to do, Violette... I'll go in—open things up a bit."

This is one of the more unusual situations I've found myself in, lately—although perhaps not as odd as exchanging clothes with a total stranger in front of the Houses of Parliament.

Assia wriggled the key into the lock and turned it, opening the door. She felt cautious, without knowing why, other than that she was entering the actual—very personally so—living space of someone she hadn't known and who had not known her. She paused in the entryway, eyes sweeping the room. Colours, curiously combined: Deepest dark green, aqua, bright blue; persimmon-red shone on the far wall—the trim on the windowsills glossy and luminous light green. Colours Assia hadn't before seen put one beside the other. She navigated around a bicycle propped against the door to the entryway closet and set the flowers and painting next to the wall in the entry hallway.

A working table, contrived from what seemed at first sight to be a vintage French door set across an iron framework, held space off-center in the room, the grid of the door's small paned windows gleaming in satiny yellow. A gorgeously trailing spider plant lofted the desk, the variegated greenery was held, suspended, from a periwinkle-twined loop that braided through a silver catch in the ceiling. Tiny, green-leafed spider plant offshoots skimmed stacked-to-slipping papers, on the desktop.

Chairs of worn leather sat away from the walls and the bank of front windows; a chaise of tattering rattan reclined in front of shelves running the length of the far wall, filled to overflow with books. The couch, blanketed in rich vanilla-coloured canvas, reposed in the middle of the room—an island of meringue floating beneath a pale turquoise sky. Assia stared into the coved ceiling, her curiousity sparked: *What is that solacing color?*

Assia walked slowly into the main room, inhaling deeply. *Jasmine... is that it?* She stepped to the front windows, looking down two levels into the small courtyard bordered with wrought iron fencing. A large tree held center, its leaves yet drifting in this very latest part of fall. *Black Maple,* Assia thought... *Does England have Black Maple trees?* Its yellow leaves wandered lazily in a pocket of blue-lit sky floating in the midst of gray damp. Assia returned her gaze to the inside of Celia's flat. Words painted on the wall scrolled beneath the row of windows:

IT FELL. BLUE LIGHT FELL FROM HER POCKET IN THE MORNING WHEN SHE RAN IN THE RAIN...

She turned from the windows, crossing the room to a short hallway that led to the bedroom. This felt almost too personal for Assia, yet she hoped that in being here she would be a help for Violette.

Luminous gold, and iridescent embroidery silks threaded the duvet cover, floating lusciously over the four-poster bed. Florescent orange pillows scattered the headboard. Turquoise velvet ribbons, tiny bells sewn to them, draped the tops of the tall posts of the bed. A book lay open on the bedside table, spine facing upward, holding its place for the reader—Celia. Tacked to the wall on one side of the bed was a large map. *What is it a map of?* Assia wondered, briefly scrutinizing it.

The oil painting over the dresser... a portrait of a woman in a green silk dressing gown. She recognized it: *Rossetti*, the 19th-century painter. Dante Rossetti. She could identify that much, but could remember nothing more about the particular portrait. She turned, then turned again, to the painting; the evocative intimacy riveted Assia's gaze. A sound startled her from her reverie—Violette, opening the now unlocked door to the flat.

Aesop unlocked the door to Assia's flat—walked through the angled hallway to the kitchen and opened the refrigerator. He grabbed the bottle of wine from the lower shelf, scanning for anything that might serve as dinner. Nothing. Aesop was famished.

Nate had no appetite. Hadn't for days. He'd reluctantly dragged himself to a restaurant several blocks from the hotel, but was unable to look at the menu and had left. He'd thought time to himself would help settle his mind and emotions, but if anything, he missed Celia more. Nate suddenly couldn't face his hotel room. He'd had it with hotel living—he'd been in San Francisco a mere few days, but suddenly understood that he couldn't deal with a hotel, especially while at such loose ends. Nate recalled having passed a nightclub a few blocks past. Perhaps that would take him from these thoughts that were too much with him. *I'll call Neal when I get back to my room—should've done that right away. Being alone Like This is probably not the best idea for me, right now.* He doubled back, eventually seeing the nightclub— lights on the marquee flashing orange neon. He wandered in.

Aesop wandered into Assia's small living room. He noted her laptop on the couch, and found himself drawn to it.

The music drew Nate further into the crowded club. Nate realized he hadn't taken the opportunity to hear live music for some time. He and Celia typically frequented pubs that were nothing as lively and noise-filled as this place was. The pubs were usually very low-key—basic beer-slopped floors, a bar—nothing added.

Add some things... Aesop thought he'd type something into Assia's November Novel. It seemed so without plot or structure—that he could determine, anyway—that he thought anything he might put into the story would certainly not detract. She might appreciate a boost in word count, at that.

Nate walked further into the club, eyes squinting in the dark, ears pummeled by the music's volume and raging bass. *Good to lose myself in this auditory overload,* he thought... *but not sure I'll last very long here.* He walked over to the bar to order a drink. Elbows resting on the rail running along the edge of the bar, Nate turned, looking over the crowd. *Haven't been in a bar this crazed since the first time I lived in the Bay area,* he thought. He turned back, pulling some cash from his pocket for the bartender.

"Well, hey... what's *your* name?"

Nate was taken aback. He looked around. Not sure about that overly friendly bar patron... this a gay bar, or mixed?

"Nate's the name," he said, almost relieved that the music may have drowned out his voice.

"Nate? Nate's your name... really... Well, that's..."

Nate decided this was enough for one night. He wasn't ready for the world of people much at all. This was overdose. Too much stimulation. Too chaotic. He left his drink on the bar and found his way, through the mash of close bodies, to the exit.

He wondered if he was in the wrong crowd, or the wrong frame of mind; he couldn't get a sense of things.

Aesop couldn't get a sense of things in Assia's novel. Assia was continually discovering unexpected story lines, according to her near-daily updates to him. Aesop scanned through the last several pages. It seemed half the characters were leaving the country for varying, who knows what, reasons. *Where were they all going?* He sifted idly through the words.

Violette sifted idly through the papers on Celia's desk. Ah! Celia's handwriting... Violette's vigilant containing of her grief was caught unawares. Tears jumped to her eyes, spilling, slipping from her cheeks, dripping onto Celia's papers, splattering the unopened mail, falling over the glass paperweight—the glassed globe with rose petals suspended within, Celia's favorite. Violette pulled out the desk chair and sat down. She pushed her hair from her face with both hands, then rested her cheek on the center stack of papers on Celia's desk, tears flowing, dissolving her carefully constructed armor. *How can I let these tears take her away from me?*

Assia picked up the book on Celia's night table—*Canterbury Tales*, Chaucer. *Chaucer... That's the dog's name, isn't it? Didn't Violette say something about "Chaucer," her dog? Odd little synchronicity.* She'd not read Chaucer in any of the Lit classes she'd taken. Assia noted the page number the book was opened to—224. Barely halfway through. The writing was in Middle English. Difficult going. Assia perused the page. *Where had she left off? What was yet to be read?*

She set the book down, careful to preserve the page the book had been opened to. Holding place—

She turned, slowly... glanced to the open closet door, catching the scent of jasmine, again. *Or was it?* Clothes hanging in a neat row: velvet jackets, cotton shirts in fuchsias and blue-grays, checks and stripes, skirts with pleats and short layers, one with sequins scattered through the fabric. *So very intimate, looking into someone else's closet— all of her things here... but then, of course her things are here... It isn't as if this woman, Celia, had just taken a vacation—she died. There are probably dishes in the sink, mail in the slot...*

Assia pulled her eyebrows down in thought: *where would a person begin? What would Violette's friend—Celia, that is—what would she want? What does one do with someone else's... life?*

Assia could hear Violette, in the living room, crying... *A good thing...* letting the tears go... into the *lacrimae rerum,* "the tears that are in all things." Assia's cell phone vibrated, flashing the message icon. *Aesop.*

Neal had no idea Nate was in the Bay area. *Where was he staying? Some bleak high-rise hotel, most likely.* They'd kept sporadic email contact. Now and then Neal had asked about Violette, through Nate, not wanting to email her directly. The parting between Violette and Neal had been painful for each of them. Neal thought if he had direct contact with Violette, things could get confusing again. He didn't want that for himself, or for her. Besides, he'd heard from Nate that she'd gotten married— precipitously, or so it had seemed—a couple of years ago.

Nate... Neal wondered if it was too late to call, yet tonight... *Maybe I'll chance leaving a voicemail. Hope I don't wake him, if he's getting any sleep... probably needs sleep more than just about anything.* He wanted Nate to have some connect to him as soon as Nate awakened, thinking his friend may be in tough shape since the death of his girlfriend. Especially after wandering around the city on his own, for a few days—no one to talk to. He could pick that up pretty clearly in Nate's voice, in the message he'd left. Neal didn't know too much about that relationship, other than that they'd been seeing one another for over a year or so. *Tragic, that explosion.* Even though it was Election Day in the U.S., it had still made significant news in the papers. *Investigation still going on,* he thought.

Aesop was at loose ends. Assia was not picking up her cell; it was getting late. He pushed himself back from her desk.

Violette pushed herself back from Celia's desk. She wiped the tears from her cheeks with the heel of her hand, sighed, and then took in a wider view of this room that was so familiar to her. Her eyes swept upward gazing into the blue of Celia's ceiling— *angels sighing blue.* Celia had named the colour. Celia's unique colour sense... Throughout her childhood, Celia was unaware that most others did not see things, colours, in ways that she did. It wasn't until she was well into adulthood that someone had told her that this ability, this quality—*what would one call it?*—had a name—*synesthesia.* Something found more commonly among novelists, painters, and poets. *A mixing—an intermingling—of the senses,* Celia would explain to others, if they were curious:

"It's about neurons, that early on in one's brain development, were supposed to disentangle—

130

and deciding not to—thereby, blending sensory elements."

Her father's cello playing spun deep hues in Celia's mind. Letters and numbers had distinct colours; Celia could decipher scent from colours, as well. Violette understood at once. Words were infused with colour in her mind. She often memorized addresses or phone numbers by colour. Celia did not bat an eyelash when Violette had said about Celia's flat number: "Four... very nice... Four is my favorite colour." But then Celia already knew that.

How had Celia come to name this colour she'd chosen for her ceiling, "angels sighing blue"—?... never thought to ask her. . . What was it she used to say about that?

"When I lie on the couch and look up at this blue, it's like holy water raining down on me."

"Violette, how are you managing—okay?" That word again, "okay." Violette thought she'd love to be "okay" sometime again, in her life.

"Yes... Let's perhaps leave, now. D'you mind?"

"Not at all. Violette, I'd be happy to help you with Celia's things. I could come back tomorrow—or whenever seems right to you—and begin packing some things. This has to be all too much for you. I can't imagine. Naturally, I'll set aside Celia's more personal belongings for you to look through, when you can manage that. Perhaps she has family, siblings, who would want some of these items as well. But in the meantime, I could take care of the more obvious things."

"Yes, yes." Violette sighed again. "Of course. I appreciate this more than I can say, being able to put trust in a near stranger. I insist on paying you for your time."

"I couldn't accept money for this," said Assia. "Wouldn't think of such a thing. I'm just so sorry that we find ourselves in this so-sad circumstance."

Assia pulled her cell phone from her pocket, to call Aesop.

"Assia! I've been worried about you. Where are you? I'm just now getting food to take back to the flat."

"So sorry, Aesop. I didn't want to call while with Violette. She's having such a hard time of it, though what would one expect? I need to get on the underground—I'm near the station now. I'll meet you at the flat... forty-five minutes or so. Would you pick up some food for me, while you're at it? I'm famished. No chance to eat, and food is not a priority for Violette right now. In fact, I tried to get her to have dinner with us but, of course, she wouldn't. Poor alone thing! Although maybe being alone is what she needs tonight. By the way, E., I need to talk to you about something."

"Okay, Assh—let me get this food ordered. We'll talk when you get here."

Aesop picked up the take-out food, and began the walk back to Assia's flat.

Assia stepped into the underground station.

Nate slept, in his hotel room.

Neal left a message for Nate, his bereft friend.

Stephen tapped Violette's number into his cell phone.

Violette turned the key to Celia's flat, locking the door behind her.

Simon moved on.

Jean-Oscar raced through the streets of London on his skateboard, connected to Chaucer by the gold leash.

And on Assia's desk, in her November Novel, Aesop's words scattered down the page:

A new character entered the scene in the November Novel of the very talented author, Assia Greene. The character's name began with an "A"—and though this character was somewhat of a mystery to the other characters in November Novel (not to be confused with the character in the novel whose name was actually "Mystery") the author was quite familiar with him. He knew that sometimes Ms. Assia Greene thought "A" was an antagonist, because that's what he'd told her when she'd asked. But the truth is, he has a very important message to deliver to Assia, the writer of **November Novel, by Assia Greene**. *A message Like This:*

I accept your proposal.

CHAPTER X.
AQUAMARINE

Nate awakened to the blinking of his cell phone. Neal's message.

"Nate, pal—so sorry about all this, man... really rough. Seriously, Nate, what can I do, buddy? I'm just heading in to work. Come downtown to the office... we'll grab lunch. I can get out of there for a couple of hours. We'll go down to the wharf, look at the water, get some shellfish. I want to hear it. All of it, Nate. Whatever you want to tell me. Whatever you need, pal— I'm right here. You're not alone... Look, Nate, buddy—should I just come by and pick you up? That's the better plan. I'll check in at work, and then come to your hotel. You hold tight, pal. I'll be there."

Nate played Neal's message through three times, comforted by his friend's voice as much as the words. Neal was the friend he'd thought to call first, when he finally felt he might be able to put words to this grief. He knew he could count on Neal for the sensitivity he yearned for. He'd no longer need to hold this alone. *Jeez, it'd be a relief to talk openly about Celie.* He couldn't do that at home, and Violette was still in shock. He hoped Violette could find someone to talk to. He knew she'd split from Simon right after the accident. Didn't know about that timing, but Celia had said something about it that he hadn't paid too much attention to at the time. Some sort of unhappiness Violette felt with Simon. He didn't know the guy. He recalled thinking at the time, that it had seemed a hasty decision to marry, as Celia had later described it—but what did he know about it all?

He recalled Violette's happiness with Neal. He'd met Violette through Neal, in fact—and was then introduced to Celia through Violette, at the Tate Gallery. He hadn't known Neal to have had a relationship with a woman, ever. Really threw him. Odd, when he thought about it. The being gay didn't surprise him or shock

136

him. It was Neal's being with Violette—that was the surprise. *Of course, things got into a mess fairly fast. A gay man becoming involved with a woman... and then Violette... What had she been feeling?* He didn't think it was his business, but now he was sorry he hadn't paid more attention—maybe been more of a friend to Neal during that time.

He'd hardly gotten to know Violette, but when he was asked by his company to transfer to the London branch for an indefinite period of time, he'd looked her up. A long way to Celia, all this, when he thought about it.

And if being with Violette was unusual for Neal, Nate's having developed a relationship with Celia was similarly out of character. In the course of his ten-year marriage, Nate had never had an affair—if that's what this was—and hadn't thought about it. He saw himself as a focused "hands on" dad. And marriage went with that, of course. He and his wife, Lauren, had grown increasingly distant, somewhere in the months after the twins were born. He'd heard that parenthood brought huge adjustments. They'd been overwhelmed with the two girls, that part was true. But things had never gotten back on track with them. Or on any track at all. He wondered now and then if Lauren could possibly be happy. Although he knew the idea of his having a relationship with anyone else was out of the question. She would never sanction that, of course, and he understood. *Why did I think Celie was not that? Not an affair? But of course she wasn't.*

Assia had no time to get to her November Novel today, which would put her back by at least 1700 words. She hated to get behind Like This. She and Aesop ate their take-out Thai food, his favorite—something she ate when hungry enough to eat anything, which she was, now, after her long day.

"Assia, we need to talk about going back, you know," Aesop said.

"I know, I know..." Assia trailed off, looking up at nothing in particular—the corner of the ceiling. She sighed.

"That's what I wanted to talk to you about... I've been thinking, E. I know this is hard to... envision—but I'd like to stay on a bit and help get Celia's flat sorted through, for Violette's sake. I suppose she could hire someone to do it. But, I felt a connection there, to the place. The colours, the items she had here and there. I don't really know how to explain it. I want to go back there, anyway. What do you think, E? I don't want you to be disappointed. And I can't really imagine what it would be like for me to be here without you."

Aesop had been afraid of just this sort of thing. In the last week, he'd been all too aware of the change in Assia. She was no longer weighted with the *angst* she'd struggled with in the weeks and months before they'd come to England. She seemed lighter in spirit. London, or England, or just being away—he wasn't sure what was making the difference. He felt the pull London had on Assia.

He reached for her. "Assh..." She leaned into him, then pushed her hand back through his hair, looked him in the eyes, and swept her gaze over his face. She loved Aesop's face.

"I could see this coming," Aesop said. "I don't want to go back to D.C. and leave you here, either. I could try to extend things in the London office but I'd like to get back to D.C. I hadn't planned to stay in London any longer than what we'd initially arranged, and I have so many things I need to attend to at home."

"Look, E, why don't you go back without me, and then we'll figure it out. I can stay on for a bit, however long it takes me, and then join you. I need to get back as well. My job! I don't know what they'd think if I didn't come back as scheduled." She pulled her eyebrows downward. "I'll email later tonight—see what I can negotiate." Assia relaxed into Aesop, decided she couldn't think about all of these things tonight. Too much emotion and... weirdness, for lack of a better word, she thought, for one day. She couldn't even face logging on to November Novel—though she was intensely curious what her characters might be up to.

"I've been thinking about heading out earlier, Assia—changing my flight so I can deal with what I need to in D.C.—clear things with my work there, to get ready for the upcoming change in administration. Obama will bring energy to the city that I can't recall seeing, ever. I want to get involved. My project here is ready to turn over to the lawyers in the London office, anyway."

Aesop drifted in thought. *This all sounds like a plan, maybe even a logical one. But I'm not happy about leaving Assia. Too much could happen. What—? Is there something I'm afraid of? Losing her? Is that it? Assh has seemed the more dependent one. I haven't given as much thought—consciously, anyway—to my need for her.* Yet, he knew he meant what he'd said, on the pages of her November Novel.

Violette was at Gatwick. She'd called Jean-Oscar as soon as she'd gotten home from Celia's flat—making the arrangements for his care for Chaucer. She'd held it in the back of her mind since meeting Jean-Oscar, seeing his obvious joy in Chaucer, and equally as importantly, observing his competence in handling the lively Chaucer—that perhaps she could leave Chaucer in the boy's care—and find some time away from London. She'd met Jean-Oscar's parents the day after meeting the lad, when he'd called to see if he could take Chaucer on a run. They seemed to adore Chaucer with the same instantaneous affection she'd witnessed in Jean-Oscar.

She'd take her chances with getting a seat on a flight that night to the States, and would book a connecting flight when she got there. Violette called for a taxi and then gathered clothes somewhat haphazardly, stuffing them into a bag. She was scattered and upset. Anxiety flooded her. Being in Celia's flat had opened her to grief's core. She hadn't thought much past getting on a plane, and soon. Her hastily concocted idea was to find a hotel room when she arrived in San Francisco, until she could figure out a better plan. She needed to be away from London. She needed to be in the sun. She needed to see the Golden Gate Bridge. She needed.

Nate turned his face to the sun's warmth. It was "jacket weather," but much warmer and more forgiving than London this time of year where the damp and cold went through skin, settling in the bones.

Neal had parked a ways from the wharf, planning to get in a good walk with Nate. They ambled, in no particular hurry, without speaking—relaxed in one another's company, as true friends are, even when they haven't seen one another for some length of time.

A different sort of urbanscape than London, Nate thought... *Less dense, less intense, brighter, another angle to the light.*

They entered the restaurant district.

"Okay, pal, talk to me," Neal said, "... and none of that macho-guy crap. Just tell me. You know me; you know I can hear it, anything you need to say. You haven't had anyone to talk to about this woman—Celia. Right? I mean, it was a secret in your marriage, obviously. Celia was Violette's best friend... I remember that. Is that how you met her?"

Neal led them to the outdoor seating area of a restaurant, pulled up an adjacent chair for Nate, and settled himself at the table. He picked up the menu absentmindedly but didn't look at it. His eyes were on his friend. A waiter ambled over and narrated an impossibly long list of specials. Nate's eyes clouded. Neal looked up at the waiter.

"Hey, yeah... we'll both take the mussels and shrimp special, and some of that sourdough bread. Bring us a loaf of that, if you would, please—oh, and a couple of beers—whatever's on tap. And some nachos to start with."

This is going to be one salty, alcohol-drenched lunch, Nate thought, wondering if Neal would get back to work this afternoon. Neal handed the menu to the waiter. Nate put his hands together and rested his forehead on them, then looked up at Neal.

"Don't know what to say. Celie. Not even sure I've said her name out loud since then. Celie was... She..." Nate faltered. "I met her at the Tate Gallery in London, when Violette was working there. I'd decided to grab a quick lunch with her. Violette, that is—she being the only person I knew in London, and I hardly knew her. Turns out Celia worked there, at the Tate, and Violette was helping her on a project. Can't remember what project, exactly—something to do with some painter or another. The family had not yet come over. A big move, and we weren't all that sure about it. I was there ahead of them. Maybe you remember all that.

"I didn't know if I'd keep up with Violette. I'd contacted her because I'd wanted to meet with someone who was familiar with the city, to help me 'ground' myself. And of course, I'd wanted to look her up because of your relationship with her. I know it was important, man." Nate drifted...

"Celia... Celia Brennan-Garrick." She held her hand to his—the ring on her index finger catching Nate's eye—a square aquamarine, bordered with tiny iridescent stones that sparked prisms of light.

"Nate Hawkins." He shook Celia's hand, commented on the ring.

"Your ring... diamonds—is that it?—bordering the blue? I don't usually notice things like that," he said.

"Yes, diamonds... that's correct. It was my grandmother's ring, actually," said Celia. "She gave it to me, of all her granddaughters, because, as she said, I was the only one who wouldn't change the setting." She smiled. "She was right, of course. Why would I?... I've no idea if it's valuable, or not, really. Now and again, I've thought to have it appraised— the diamonds, you know. It's valuable to me, though, because she was. She died nearly sixteen years ago, just a few months after I'd married. The last time I saw Gram was at my wedding. Sixteen years... and I miss her every day. Why I didn't think to save more than a handful of her letters, I'll never understand. I suppose I didn't let myself imagine she'd be gone so soon. A regret, you know. Hand-written letters are a rarity, now. And then of course I'm just going on and on Like This and only having just met you. Let's go then, shall we? And have some tea. Or perhaps you prefer coffee? I'll show you the exhibit Violette and I have been working on."

"Violette had to get going and Celia said she'd show me around the Gallery. I went back every day after that. What can I say? It's not like I'd ever done this sort of thing, or even thought about it—seeing another woman every day like that. Hey, I know some guys do. I suppose women, too, for that matter, but I just didn't. Anyway... somehow it all seemed outside of my normal life. Maybe all guys who have—well, *affairs* I guess is the word— think that. I don't know.

"I never thought of it as an affair because I never thought of myself that way. Still don't, and I don't—didn't—think of Celie that way. I'm rambling. Can't figure out what I'm saying... I'd meet her at her work—the Tate, that is—and have lunch with her. It took a while before I realized we were, you know, 'seeing' each other. She showed me different exhibits and paintings— the Turners, I recall—sea paintings—not that I like water all that much. You know that about me... and the modern pieces she liked. Art galleries have never been 'my thing,' either. You know that, too. But I was falling for Celia. I loved watching her, listening to her. She was just... " Nate put his head in his hands. Neal looked at him. Waited. "I can't believe she's gone! We were so... so intimate—I... and not in the way you might think, hard to explain. I got so fucking close to her. I've never felt that close to anyone... She said she thought of me as 'hers,' that every now and then she remembered I had a wife and a family somewhere, but that she really thought we were together.

"It was hard for her to have me leave at night. I didn't stay the night with her, ever. A regret. Couldn't, of course. By the time she and I were close like that, the family was here. Lauren

143

and I had rented a place outside of London. Really hard for Celie when I would leave—like I said. Got to be hard for me, also. Ah, Neal, what can I say? Can't figure out how to manage it. At all. I try not thinking about her and that seems to be all I can do. Think about her. And miss her."

Neal looked at his friend for a long moment.

"Nate... *Miss her*... Miss her as goddamned much as you want. You loved her. She deserves your missing her Like This. Even though it fucking hurts like hell. Jeez, Nate, I'm so fucking sorry. I'm sure you don't want to hear this right now, but you've been lucky. Blessed. Whatever you want to call it, to have ever loved someone that way."

Nate closed his eyes against the heart hurt, dropped his head to the table, his hair falling over his forehead. Neal got up from his chair and walked around the table to sit next to his grieving friend. Neal put his arm around Nate. No words. After a long moment, Nate lifted his head. Neal looked him directly in the eyes.

"Nate. Buddy... You'll get yourself back, friend. It takes time. Lots of time. Need to hang out with friends who can hear it, or at least be there with you while you walk yourself through. Wish I could say something useful..." Tears came to Nate's eyes. Finally, he let them come.

"Eat some of this food, Pal..." Neal pushed a plate toward Nate. "I've over-ordered as usual. Let's get started on these beers. The rest of the day will be what it is. We'll just hang with it. I'm really glad you're here, Nate. Don't be alone with this kind of stuff. It's too fucking much. Just too fucking much."

CHAPTER XI.

INDIGO, REDUX

Stephen could not get through to Violette on her cell. He decided to try email. Not exactly what he wanted, but it'd have to do.

Violette was sitting at JFK airport, weary beyond all telling. She sat at the gate awaiting her connecting flight, flipping through a *New York Times* absentmindedly, not reading any of it. She thought vaguely about how to arrange work. She thought she could extend the leave she was on, knowing the school personnel would understand. But finances were going to get tight, too tight, and soon—if she didn't sort herself out. Celia, Simon, her marriage. She was relieved the twins were off for a month's vacation and taken care of. She knew her parents to be up to the task of taking them on for a while, as she was not right now. Perhaps she and Simon could sell the house. They most likely would have to do that anyway, given that she wanted to divorce. Money would be an issue.

Assia slept restlessly, awakening to thoughts of Aesop's departure that may be as soon as tomorrow. He'd had too many arrangements to make to stay with Assia for the night. She didn't know what to think about his leaving—couldn't imagine not seeing Aesop each day. They were best friends—connected heart, body, and soul. Aesop had international cell phone connection capabilities on his phone, as did she. Yet an entire ocean between them seemed too far. She got up, pulled on her sweatshirt for quick warmth, and wandered around the flat trying to gather herself together. *I'll get coffee going, and then start in on that word count for November Novel.* She'd missed a day. *Wonder what these characters are up to now?*

Assia sat at her desk, set her coffee to the side, and logged-on. She scrolled for her place, and caught the words that had been typed in a font other than the one she used. *What's this? Ah... I see. Aesop must've gotten on here. Hope he put in a good 1700 words... Unlikely.* Assia read through Aesop's paragraph. She sat back in her chair, tapped her fingers on the desk, picked up her coffee cup and, holding it with both hands, blew over it, watching the steam mist her computer screen.

Stephen emailed Violette: ***Violette—tried calling cell but could not get through. I don't know how you are since Celia... and all... am worried about you. I'd like to see you. I wonder if you'd consider that—Stephen.***

Aesop was up early, ready to pack. He could catch a flight later in the afternoon if he could get things set with the flat and with work. A lot to take care of. He wasn't sure he could get the details managed, and still pack in time for the early evening flight. Once he'd decided to leave without Assia, he wanted to get to it. He felt almost frantic. Not a good feeling-state from which to make major plans. The airlines had said he could have a seat on the red-eye to New York, but he needed to decide soon; there were only a few seats left. The connecting flight would leave the following day.

Neal offered to put Nate up, indefinitely, until Nate could figure out what he wanted to do. Neal had a reasonably sized apartment, but Nate didn't want to impose.

> Violette re-read Stephen's email.
> Nate re-considered Neal's offer.
> Aesop re-checked the airlines.
> Assia re-read Aesop's *November Novel* insertion.

Violette said no to Stephen's offer—thought a moment more, and said—yes.

Nate said no to Neal's offer—thought a moment more, and said—yes.

Aesop told the airlines no—thought a moment more, and said—yes.

And as to the statement posed to her, in her November Novel, by a Mr. A. Wind-Rivers, the author, Assia Greene, said, "*What* proposal?"

Chaucer was worn out. He and Jean-Oscar had been traversing the business district of London pell-mell, skateboard-to-roller-blades. Home again, Chaucer lay down and fell into a sound sleep. Jean-Oscar, not far behind, settled himself in bed, turned off the light, and pulled the covers up to his chin.

Assia left a message for Aesop on his cell: "Aesop... I forgot to tell you... I've been thinking about something, since being in Celia's flat..."

Rain fell intermittently. The daylight hours shortened. The air grew chill and damp. The fog lay heavy.

Aesop moved back into his row house in Washington D.C.

Nate moved into Neal's spare bedroom.

Violette moved into a hotel room in San Francisco.

Chaucer and Jean-Oscar moved into the London home of Jean-Oscar and his parents, Elodie Millieniers and Claude De La Ponte.

And Assia moved into Celia's flat, in London.

Assia didn't know where to begin. She wasn't sure she'd be ready to return to America to live, at least not just yet. She rather liked living here, in London, and hoped to find a way to support herself, and to try to write more. *For a while, at least. Would Aesop consider coming back to England for an extended time? Hard to say. Most likely—unlikely.* The flat—Celia's—that needed some deciding as well. What to leave. What to be given—and to whom, and where. How to make a home for herself in this flat that belonged to another.

Assia wondered how Violette would feel about her decision to move into Celia's flat. She hardly knew Violette, and though she liked her—a lot, even—it was hard to tell what kind of friendship, if any, might develop. The day after Assia and Violette had been in Celia's flat, Violette surprised Assia with a phone message saying that she was leaving for the States—California. From the breathlessness in Violette's voice in the message, Assia was left with the impression that Violette was a bit shocked by the decision herself. Without an international cell phone connection for Violette, Assia didn't have communication with her. *Perhaps I can get her email address from Simon. If I can track Simon down, that is.*

Violette arrived in San Francisco in the early morning, the fog still blanketing the bay. How she'd managed her best night's sleep since Celia's death, she couldn't fathom. Perhaps it was the intensity of her fatigue and the backlog of sleepless nights. This morning she'd felt a heartbeat of energy. Her idea was to find a hotel, some breakfast, and get herself sorted out a bit. She had an ambitious plan to find an art supplies store and set herself up somewhere near the Golden Gate Bridge. She wanted to make good on her promise to Celia to complete a painting of that magnificent bridge. Anticipating being near the bridge again flashed hope in Violette to her very core—a feeling she'd not experienced for some time. She couldn't have said when.

It was Violette who saw Neal, in line at the Pier.

It was Nate who saw the painting, of Celia.

It was Aesop who saw the front window display, of:

November Novel, by Assia Greene.

It was Jean-Oscar who saw the woman wearing the hajib.

And it was Chaucer who saw the jeans. Assia's jeans.

CHAPTER XII.

IRIDESCENCE

Violette found Paint or Dye Art Supply along a side street, several blocks from the Pier. She'd gotten the name from someone at the hotel she'd checked into and, to her surprise, had been able to find it in the tangle of streets. Violette wandered among rows of canvases stacked twenty deep against walls, floor-to-ceiling shelves of glistening paint tubes, the banded labels denoting colours along arrays—one colour per row. Overwhelmed, she stood back and perused the tracks of colours, gradually reaching for tubes of oil paint by any colour that intuitively resonated for her.

She stood on tiptoe. Spying a stepladder next to the wall, she pulled it to the shelves. Balancing close to the topmost step of the ladder, she reached her fingers to the shelves, choosing the palest shades of gold, soft blues, pinks, yellowy-greens, whites, and red, orange, deep purple. Cerulean. She'd packed so hastily for the trip that she'd brought none of her art materials. She decided to purchase an easel that could be set up outside, and brushes—whatever she thought she'd need. She was doing this for Celia; she was not going to worry so, over cost.

Nate slept later than usual in Neal's comfortable guest bed. He set himself up in Neal's sunlit living room, with coffee and the *San Francisco Chronicle*. He'd always liked the tactile feel of this particular newspaper and was pleased to find it had not changed. The *Chronicle* was printed on paper that was thinner—less inky, than that of the *London Daily* or *New York Times*. Like California air in a way. Lighter.

This, the first morning since the accident that he could recall awakening with energy, inspired Nate. He might get out for a run yet, and perhaps some work on his November Novel.

Hmmm... Nate thought he should be at thirty thousand words by now. He remembered being somewhere in the twenty thousands. If he were actually ten thousand words behind, he'd add another thousand to his daily quota. He'd have to get the story line going so the words would race. He had no idea where he'd left off. He remembered how amazed Celie was that he had chapters. He couldn't imagine proceeding any other way. Her writing, of course, was all flow.

Nate balanced the coffee mug on the arm of the couch and looked toward the floor-to-ceiling bay window of the east wall. Sun. Neal's apartment was the top floor of an old Victorian house, this upper apartment, spacious, of comfortable dimensions; it felt contained, perimetered by full windowed light on four sides. Nate could see Neal's eye in the furnishings: Neal loved texture— like the dark green velvet couch Nate was sitting on. *Holding up well, I see,* Nate observed, running his hands over the ribbed-textured surface. Neal had had the couch for years. Nate had been with Neal when Neal had discovered this couch... *in that unusual little shop. What was the name of that place?*—tucked in amongst some buildings off a side street they'd ambled along, on a lazy lunch hour. *Some painter's name—that shop... Rossetti! That was it—Dante Rossetti. The shop was called Dante's... something or other.* Hard to struggle for words, or complete memories... Maybe it would come to him. He'd ask Neal if he remembered the name of that shop.

Celie had a print of a Rossetti in her bedroom—on the wall above her dresser, opposite the wall with the map... The map of... What the heck was that map of? Why can't I recall that? She'd turn her head to look at it, from the bed—put her index finger on it and trace along a line—when they were lying next to one another on the bed, close, *clothes-on intimacy*—an intimacy he'd not known with another. *That so comfortable and right place—as if there were all the time in the world—for us.*

Nate had lived with Neal briefly in another apartment in the city, years ago—when Neal was launching his latest bread-baking business. Neal had contracted with Nate's consulting firm to help with the business expansion. People understandably confused their names. Neal had lived in the third-floor apartment of this Victorian House for several years now—most recently with his partner of a year or more. Neal's emails had been full of talk of him... *Bennett. That was the name.* The break-up had been initiated by Neal—he knew that much, but didn't know how that had come to be. Nate was sorry he hadn't been in contact with Neal more frequently during that time.

Nate pulled on his running shoes, found the spare key—still kept on the hook in the coat closet where he'd remembered it; he let himself out. He walked down the front walkway, morning sun washing over him. *Like holy water...* Coming to California was a good decision, he thought. He felt a bit better today. In spite of the missing pieces in his memories, his thinking had a clarity that had been lacking since he'd been in the hospital, struggling toward consciousness. He didn't want to think about that. Not now. Nate looked into the azure sky, inhaled iridescent light.

Violette had set herself up with a view of the bridge. *Yes... I've definitely missed filling myself all-the-way-to-full, with the sight of this bridge. Impossible beauty.* She started to squeeze paints onto her palette. Looked. The bridge stood against a backdrop of sapphire sky—*a saturation of blue that makes a person's heart hurt.*

All right then, how to start? A sigh caught Violette's breath and swept through her heart, bringing the sting of sudden tears—Chaucer... Ah... how she missed him! Right this minute. She knew he was in good hands with Jean-Oscar, although it had been a quick decision to leave Chaucer with him. She'd since talked with Jean-Oscar's parents, who, in very limited English-mixed-to-French, had reassured her that Chaucer was fine. Yet, to have him with her on such a gorgeous day... Chaucer would be so very happily distracted with the high-spirited roller-bladers, in particular.

Violette had emailed Stephen to let him know how to locate Chaucer—asking Stephen to check on the pooch and to send her updates, via email—a means to keep tabs on how Chaucer was getting on. She missed Stephen, still—and was happy to have some sort of connection Like This, though she wasn't sure how wise it was for her—contacting Stephen again. She had to keep herself from wanting more, and didn't find it easy to be careful enough to prevent that. The feelings of desire for him had not gone away. *Why is it I can be this attached to a man who would not be fully present in my life?* She couldn't sort it through. The connection he sought with her, intermittently, would catch her up, again and again. *Intermittent reinforcement*—the "never really gone away," the "not predictably there." Hard to let go of, truly. She'd had to put mind over heart to actually break from him and hold to it, this last time.

Assia turned the key in the lock. This time, standing on the threshold felt quite different for her. She was entering a flat she'd be making her home in—the home of a woman whose belongings were still there, in place—lingerie in drawers, jewelry on dresser top, book half-read opened to the page last left off... *no doubt, food, still in the refrigerator and cupboards. What will I find here, in this flat? What will I find in myself, in living here? That's the bigger question.*

She remembered putting the key in another lock, much Like This one, a few years ago—to the brownstone on *Jenifer Street, Washington D.C.*—*cars parked bumper-to-bumper tight, along both sides of the shaded street. There were no garages. Something that had taken Assia some getting used to, once she'd found herself living in the city. Made for more of a sense of community, she'd thought. It was, in fact, how she'd met Aesop, on an already-sultry Washington D.C. morning as she was leaving for the seminar she'd come to the city to attend. He'd been at the curb near to her row house, unlocking his car.*

It had been steamy hot. Assia's first day in this city—an overheated Washington D.C. day, with the heat at one hundred, and the air-quality index in the red zone. "That can't be good—the red zone," Assia thought. "Whatever it means."

Humidity lay heavy. Moisture skimmed the windows, obscuring her view as she attempted to peer in from the porch. Her bag slipped from her shoulder onto the wide floorboards, painted the color of green that Assia had seen so often on the porches of older Midwestern houses—the wide lazy front porches and the narrow back-step ones—that she'd come to think of the color as "porch green."

She'd stood on the threshold of the doorway, wiggling the unfamiliar key into the unfamiliar lock, turning it. The row house belonged to a friend-of-a-friend. She'd never met the owners. She'd paused for a moment before crossing the threshold, lifting the hair away from the back of her neck, hoping for even an illusion of coolness. She hadn't thought to ask about air-conditioning, and wasn't altogether sure that she wanted to know, now—fearing the worst. She entered, dragging her bag through the doorway, placing the house key on a small table by the door while making a mental note: "Key... doorway." The key, one thing she needed to keep track of.

Colors of young childhood greeted her: green, red, blue, and yellow. The couple had a two-year-old child, she recalled. Her eyes swept the small living room—a red ball with silver stars, Legos® built into a blue and green tower, bright yellow plastic cylinder cups of Play-Doh®. She lifted the lid on the container of turquoise Play-Doh, inhaling. Scent-memory.

Puzzles, children's books, adult books. More books. And more. The living room connected directly to the kitchen, where bookshelves tucked into walls and corners of every small space; a tall, narrow shelf, crowded with books, squeezed in next to the kitchen table. The living room library shelves, full-to-bursting with precariously perched books, at-the-ready to slip, intrigued Assia. She thought she might forego the seminar she'd come to D.C. to attend, and instead simply stay in this lovely old brownstone to read. She noticed a thermostat on the kitchen wall, and hoped she could figure the correct sequence of buttons to elicit cool air.

Her eye scanned titles of poetry, art, and metaphysics. The Soul of the Night, Chet Raymo—a favorite of Assia's. She eased a book from the tight grasp of the jammed-in row of books, carefully, to prevent avalanche: The Gift:"Creativity and the Artist in the Modern World," by Lewis Hyde, setting it on the table next to The House of Life, Dante Rossetti. A book nearly sliding off the shelf's edge onto a slouchy chair below: Portrait of a Lady, Henry James. She'd been looking for that very book, intending to look up the quote she'd had on her mind these weeks, post separation from her marriage. She sank into the chair's depths, lifted her feet onto the child's table to a spot between finger paints and Legos, and began to peruse the book. It took a bit of looking but she came to it: p. 445:

> **"I must go to England,"** she said with a full consciousness that her tone might strike an irritable man of taste as stupidly obstinate.
>
> **"I shall not like it if you do,"** Osmond remarked.
>
> **"Why should I mind that? You won't like it if I don't. You like nothing I do or don't do. You pretend to think I lie."**

Isabel's broken heart. Assia's opening heart.

Assia's eyes traversed the room to the painted white upright piano against the far wall, hazed light from the front window shadowing the keys. She pulled herself from the cushioned depths of the easy chair and moved to the piano bench; she opened the children's songbook, found on the top of the piano—propped it open, and played "Lavender's Blue," "Baby's Bed's a Silver Moon," and then played "Amazing Grace," three times.

Assia entered Celia's flat—her new home—quietly, as though she might disturb someone. She looked around the small entryway, the painting still against the wall where she'd left it the other day, when here with Violette. Coat hooks catching jackets tossed to them, haphazardly—sleeves, still carrying Celia's imprint. *Odd that inanimate objects—cast-off clothing, most especially—can hold a person's presence.* She set the few things she'd carried in from the MINI, on the chair by the window. Celia's MINI. Assia had gotten the car keys from the flat, when here with Violette. Violette had encouraged Assia to use Celia's MINI while in London. It would certainly come in handy for her now. Though, getting used to the steering wheel on the right was "throwing" her. She and Aesop hadn't driven much at all in England, public transportation and taxis taking care of their needs quite nicely.

Aesop! I need to remember to call him... She wasn't sure about his arrival times in D.C., nor the calculation of time difference. She missed him, already. With Violette gone, she was quite alone. She'd met very few people really, having had Aesop with her, and having been busy with her writing. Her writing— another thing she needed to attend to, and soon. She didn't like getting more than one day behind on the word count November Novel required, having learned her lesson in starting this venture three days behind schedule—those three days necessitating her playing catch-up for nearly a week. Assia tossed her bag on the couch and went into the kitchen, with high hopes for coffee.

Violette's painting mystified her. It didn't look like the bridge at all. In any way. In fact, the painting she'd gotten a start on while positioned in front of the Houses of Parliament looked more like the Golden Gate Bridge. Now that she was looking right at the bridge, her painting looked like—*what?* She couldn't tell. She tipped her head to the side, set her brush down, and tapped her chin with her finger. It did look like something... some *one*, actually. It seemed to resemble *a face. Why would that be?*

Violette tried mixing more rusts, reds, oranges, and golds, into her palette—yet, couldn't get the bridge's colour. She was drawn to putting her brush into the paler colours and pinks. Skin tones. Tones that reminded her of someone. Skin, nearly translucent, with a fragility to it, in the pale pinks—a sweetness belying strength... *Celia.* Of course it was. It was Celia's face coming to view on the canvas.

Violette hadn't realized what she was doing until just now, standing back from it a bit—giving it a good look. She pushed a strand of hair from her cheek, looked at the painting with an artist's eye. Yes, that was truly it. Just... the hair, more gold. A lighter green in the eyes. She'd captured it. Celia's essence. The light. Her open-heartedness.

And it was too soon.

Violette started weeping. In the most public of parks, in front of that most compelling of bridges. Weeping for her own opened, broken heart that could find no release deep enough, full enough, for the loss of her friend. She set her brush on the tray of the easel and stepped away—looked at the image, wiped her sleeve across the tears on her cheeks. And thought. Violette gathered her jacket tightly around her; she sat down on the curb of the sidewalk, taking in a deep breath, a breath that reached all the way to the saddest part of her heart, infusing it with light. Benediction. She was unaware of the sun shining fully on her face, the wind lifting loose strands of her hair, winding and weaving them, gently. *What am I going to do with this painting?*

CHAPTER XIII.

BLUE

Chaucer insisted. What had gotten into him? Jean-Oscar saw more life and action in the dog each day. He was beyond happiness that he and Chaucer had met. His parents had been reluctant to take on a pet while moving between two homes—one in London, the other in Paris. Chaucer's having shown up in Jean-Oscar's life was auspicious. Jean-Oscar was thrilled that Chaucer's owner—this lovely painter woman, Violette—had needed a "Chaucer-watcher."

Jean-Oscar found himself watching *her* as well, as he and Chaucer blur-sped by, he on the skateboard, Chaucer pulling him by the leash.

Jean-Oscar thought it was the roller blades that enticed Chaucer's exuberant need for chase. *Wheels. That must be it.* He recalled that it had been the rapidly rotating wheels of his skateboard that had mesmerized Chaucer—hence, Jean-Oscar's luck in meeting the dog that had so charmed him. Jean-Oscar preferred to think Chaucer had recognized him for some reason. He thought he and Chaucer belonged to each other. Simple as that. He was quite accustomed to holding firmly to the leash whenever wheels were in motion near enough to catch Chaucer's eager eye. And Jean-Oscar himself was rather captivated by the woman. He'd never before seen a woman wearing both a *hajib*, and roller blades, on the streets of London. Though, he'd seen so many unusual things while out and about with Chaucer, he was sorry he hadn't kept a list. And Chaucer tended to pull him into scenes quite out of the ordinary.

But it wasn't the wheels, the sound they made on the pavement, or their speed or motion. Chaucer was taken with something else, something he needed to sink his teeth into—and that something else seemed to be the woman's jeans. Chaucer barked insistently, pulling at the leash, jumping towards the woman on the roller blades.

"Chaucer! *Mon Dieu!* Slow. Take it easy, my man. What's gotten into you?

"Chaucer!" Chaucer would not be deterred. Jean-Oscar turned 'round on his skateboard and let Chaucer pull him toward the woman. "*Bon jour! Je suis tres tres desole!!* I do not know what my dog is about, here. I'm ever so sorry if he's startling you!" Jean-Oscar never knew when someone might understand French. He spoke English for the most part, but was self-conscious about his accent—or, the lack thereof, as he saw it—preferring French.

"Oh no, it is fine, really. Do you understand my English? Yes? Good. Ahh!" The woman shrieked. Chaucer had put his teeth into her pants leg. Jean-Oscar could see that the jeans were already many-times-mended. Jean-Oscar had jeans similar, though not nearly as worn and wildly stitched-over. He was sure Chaucer could do real damage to these—and quickly.

"Chaucer. Bad manners, my friend. Come, Exuberant-one! Let go! Before any harm befalls. Let us be on our way!" But Chaucer would have none of it. "Chaucer!" Jean-Oscar bent down to coax Chaucer's teeth from the jeans.

"I'm so sorry. *Oh, ça alors, pas encore!* I've no idea what to do. I cannot understand this." Jean-Oscar glanced around to see if perhaps someone could help the situation, not that he knew what anyone could do for him. A couple of people approached, making varying suggestions.

"Here, let me help you. I'll hold the fellow, and you work on getting his teeth loose from the pants," said one lad. Jean-Oscar thought the woman a good sport, given that she had a dog attached to her clothing. As Jean-Oscar pulled harder on Chaucer's mouth, Chaucer's teeth ripped into the pants leg along the front, a large tear opening just below the knee. In moments, the rip gave way. Chaucer let go.

"I'm so sorry! Ah! I have no idea what to say. Here, let me take your name. I will write mine for you. I will figure something out. I can repay you for your pants." Jean-Oscar held Chaucer, hoping to settle him a bit, and thus preventing another jump for the jeans.

"Yes, yes, do not worry about it at all. Here, of course... I will give you my name and telephone number; however, I do not want you to be anxious in the least. I will patch them. They are, as you see, quite many times repaired as it is. No harm done." The woman was too kind. She tentatively held her hand toward Chaucer.

"Here, fellow. Something about me seems to have upset you, I see. I am not used to such friendly dogs. I am not used to dogs at all, truly." Chaucer whimpered and then jumped at the woman while Jean-Oscar reflexively pulled back on the leash. The woman stepped quickly back.

Jean-Oscar was nonplussed. "I am so sorry, again! Obviously, those are favorites of yours, as I can see they are—forgive me if I am being rude—they are quite... *worn*, shall we say? Unless, of course, you bought them that way. That seems to be how they are selling now."

The woman laughed. "It's an odder story that you might suppose," she said, stepping back from Chaucer's likely reach. "I came by these jeans quite by happenstance. I accidentally picked them up. They were wrapped in a package that got mixed in with other packages I had set on the floor of the coffee shop I was in. When I realized my mistake, I thought to go back to the coffee shop and simply turn them in. I thought whoever was missing them would most likely be back to the coffee shop and be able to retrieve them. But, tragically, that was the very shop that had that horrific explosion. I could not believe it. So many lives were lost that day. I cannot stop thinking about it. Well, so many of us cannot stop thinking about it. So, there you have it. I had no idea what to do. I did not even know if they were valuable to whomever they belonged to. They are just a pair of jeans, after all. Yet... I was just caught not knowing. I rather took to them and the tragically odd story." Jean-Oscar was staring up at her, still holding Chaucer, tightly.

"Yes, well that is very strange. Such a story. Again, I am sorry. I will notify the owner of Chaucer. I am Chaucer's friend and keeper. His owner is out of the country. But I will reimburse you in some way for this. Chaucer, let us be distracted, good friend. We shall get ourselves going the other way—sort out something to eat, how about that?" He led Chaucer one way and the woman backed the other direction, then turned, resuming her roller-blading.

Violette saw the email from Stephen with the word Chaucer in the title. She clicked on.

Violette—

Checked on the boy, Jean-Oscar, and charming family—the Millieners-de la Pontes—and Chaucer. Seems Chaucer got himself into bit of trouble yesterday with regard to attaching his teeth to the pants leg of a woman—someone they came past on the walkways while they were out and about. That Chaucer would not let go, and apparently, before things could be contained, had created a sizable tear in the woman's pants. Jean-Oscar says the woman was gracious about the whole thing and says the jeans, such as they were, were quite "ripped" in style, as it is. Jean-Oscar has the woman's name and cell phone number, and even though he assures me that she was not upset and did not want remuneration, the poor boy is quite stricken—wonders about providing some kind of recompense. Told him would email to you. Happy to take care of it but wanted to know if you had any particular thoughts. Hope you are doing fine in sunny California. Perhaps you and I can talk a bit when you come back to England. You are coming back?

Cheers, Stephen

Violette read Stephen's email through three times, tapped her chin, not quite believing what she was seeing.

Aesop read Assia's email. He sighed, not believing what he was seeing.

Assia read Aesop's latest email through, and then again. She put her head in her hands, not quite believing the words.

Nate walked past an Art Gallery just around off the corner at Lombard, and then stopped, turned back—unable to believe what he was looking at.

Chaucer, in the home of the Millieners-de la Pontes, turned around three times on the rug in front of the gas fireplace and settled himself down. And no one would be able to quite believe what he had seen.

Nate stared. The painting was perhaps two-feet-by-three, in dimension—*Celia. The living spirit of her.* The artist had captured the light in Celie's face that his photos could not. His eyes caught *essence*—manifest in... what? Colorations? Texture? *Must be Violette's creation. Has to be. Who else could've created this work of art? It's Celia. Definitely. How is it this painting has come to be here? Is Violette in the Bay area?* A few days out of contact with one another might've made the difference in truly knowing where she was, he thought. She may have come here, after all. *Should I buy the painting?* he thought. Did he want it? *How could I let anyone else buy it?* What would he do with an oil painting of the woman he loved when he was not actually living anywhere, not to mention that he had a marriage—such as it was—to return to? Could he bear to look at it? He could not turn away.

Aesop did not want to be reading this. Assia was staying on in London for at least the year, she said. *How could she know that?* A year seemed like quite a commitment. What about her home, and her job, in D.C.? What about their relationship? How could she think she would get along without a job, and so few contacts or friends? Moving into the flat of the woman who had died? Seemed a bit strange.

Aesop realized he was responding to this news somewhat chauvinistically. Of course, Assia would be fine. Of course, she would find some kind of income, and friends. Most likely he was afraid of losing her to her life in London. Aesop's thoughts rushed. He had to admit to himself that he missed Assia, and that he wanted her with him.

Assia had held a wild hope that Aesop would decide to come back to England. But Aesop had written that he was committed to being in Washington for the inaugural and that he fervently hoped to be part of the Obama administration in some capacity, however small—that this was history in the making, in the way that Aesop wanted history to be made. Absolutely, thought Assia. *But then where does that leave me? The two of us?* She pondered the decisions they'd made. *It doesn't have to be dramatic, does it?*

She tried to level herself. *What's a year, really?* They could travel back and forth across the ocean to see one another. *Couldn't we?*

What she would do with her loneliness was the real question. Aesop had so often held the line on that for her. She knew she needed to find a way through this deep loneliness herself. She needed to do that much, in order to trust herself.

Violette tipped her head to one side, and thought. *Could the woman have been wearing Assia's jeans? Is that possible? Why else would Chaucer so insistently attach himself to the jeans? Though admittedly lively, Chaucer was typically a well-behaved dog. If they were Assia's jeans, how was that possible?* Perhaps she'd email Stephen for the woman's phone number. She'd ask her—see what the story was. Or perhaps Jean-Oscar knew something.

Nate and Neal had dinner downtown. "No question, man, better grab that painting before it sells. If it's as captivating as you describe, someone will buy it. Front window, no less. Let's get down first thing tomorrow and see what we have. Come to think of it, it's been a long time since I've seen one of Violette's paintings... and of course, a long time since I've seen Violette. I wonder where she is—where she's staying. Give her a call, Nate. Find out why she let that go. I can keep the painting for you... why not? Hard as it may be now to look at it—you'd regret not grabbing it while you have this chance. Who knows if Violette would paint another, or get that lighting right—the way you described it." Neal looked up as the waiter approached. "Yeah, thanks—more bread, another couple of beers, more shrimp. Nate, man, are you eating a thing? Am I eating all this by myself?"

Stephen could not decode Violette's email regarding the woman and the jeans. *What was she talking about?* He looked for the card that Jean-Oscar had given him, noting the phone number. Violette would not be easily reached—it would have to be an international call. She could no doubt charge it to her hotel account, but that would not be prudent, Stephen thought. Perhaps he'd call the woman, himself, and attempt to retrieve an email contact for Violette.

Stephen thought for a moment. He didn't usually give himself moments to think. He kept busy with the full teaching schedule he'd had this term at Oxford, as well as his research and following the cricket matches that were his passion. Yet it had been different than he'd expected—this move to Oxford, his *alma mater*, to teach. He liked his students, but had been surprised to find that he missed London. His days at Oxford had been some of his happiest; yet, he couldn't find the similar sort of mood, extant, as a professor. *I suppose that makes sense— on a certain level, that is*, he thought. *Still, I'm not sure I quite expected the outright—what is it, then? Aloneness. I suppose that's it.* He surprised himself with this word.

Stephen thought about Violette. *I wonder why things didn't work out better for us...* He did miss her. And he knew she'd become strongly, emotionally attached to him. He hadn't met that attachment. *Can't think why, really. Haven't taken time to think about it at all, actually. Quite likely the problem, that—the "not taking the time."*

All right then, where is it? Stephen haphazardly sifted through the papers on his desk... *the card, with the number. Why didn't I simply put it in my wallet?* Violette had been upset with their separating, and he hadn't known what to do. *A woman like Violette...* He knew she'd wanted more time than he had to give. Or more contact. Or... *what was it she'd called it? Checking-in-with, that was it.* He had to admire her leaving the relationship, but regretted that they couldn't continue the way they had been. *Ah! Here it is:* 9 n7747 08.

He tapped the numbers on his cell phone: Several rings. A message: "Leave a message for Safia, after the tone, please." *Safia... There's a name I haven't heard.* Stephen tapped his fingers on the desktop waiting for the tone: "Yes—hello... Safia—Stephen Beckett, here. I am—ah... well, I guess one could say that I am part-owner of the dog in question—Chaucer, is his name. I have your calling card, from Jean-Oscar—the boy who was with Chaucer when you three met up. Could you ring me back please, regarding the... a... the incident? The number is 4-848440. Thank you, ever so much."

Assia wasn't sure what to do with Celia's belongings. She was able to box up some things, and then didn't know what to do with the boxed items. She'd decided to await Violette's return before actually donating anything. She knew Celia's family, in Ireland, had not wanted to retrieve anything—Celia's brother had made no claim to Celia's belongings.

Assia decided to take a break in the packing up of these belongings—clothing, dishes, paraphernalia that held no meaning for her—and yet, as she knew, may be infused with memory and experience, nuance, emotion—for the one who had chosen them—perhaps cherished them. She sighed, and rubbed her hand across the back of her neck, aching now, from the lifting and packing. She needed to get some words going on *November Novel*. She recalled seeing a robe draped across the desk chair, in the living room. Assia put her laptop next to the window, and wandered back through the short hallway to the living room.

Silk, Assia thought, as she slipped into Celia's green robe. *Gorgeous deep green. Soothing.* She looped the belt of the robe around her waist, loosely. She'd decided to work in front of the long window of the kitchen, a narrow, contained space, bordered by the stove on one side and the counter on the other. Assia moved the dish drainer to the back of the counter, and repositioned her laptop. A note slipped off the counter, from beneath the dish drainer. Assia looked at it: *Call T. Re Finances—*

A life caught in mid-sentence, completely cut off. Is that how it is? Impossible to think about.

Assia pulled the stool from beneath the counter, moving it to the window. She looked around the kitchen, her curiosity sparked. *Did Celia like to cook? Did she use her kitchen much?* No sign of cookbooks... blue china, piled high, teetered in the screened cupboards. Assia noted the unusual shape of the plates—oval, scalloped along the sides and painted with the Chinese pagoda scene depicting the poignant story of lovers precipitously parted from one another; the pair of bluebirds at the top of the scene representing their reuniting. Reunited, *somewhere in time*, Assia thought. Assia opened the cupboard and lifted the top plate from the stack, turning it over to check for an identifying label:

Old Willow
Alfred Meakin
England

Haven't heard of this maker, Assia thought.

On the shelf by the stove, glass measuring cups stacked in one another in precarious balance. *Barely used, from the looks of them*, Assia mused. Next to that, a set of bowls: green, turquoise, bright blue—nearly new. Colors—deep and bright—throughout the narrow kitchen space. Pantry cupboard, not too full: boxed soups, pastas, and tins of pates and food items unfamiliar to Assia.

No pots or pans that she could see, nor any cooking apparatus or appliances—save the electric teakettle. The teakettle, deeply patina-ed, was at least something that was obviously very much used.

Assia opened the cupboard above the sink. Wine: reds, South American. She could identify that much, even though not much of a wine connoisseur; she knew Aesop enjoyed fine wines, knowledgeable enough to take risks in trying those he was not familiar with, when dining out. Assia went along with whatever Aesop was trying, Malbec being the one name in wine that she had enough familiarity with to choose on her own.

Assia opened the wide, shallow drawer, to the left of the sink. Silverware aligned in neat rows, within. *Actual silver,* Assia noted, the initial "G" engraved on each piece. Assia felt the heaviness of true silver, in lifting a soup spoon next to her cheek. She liked the coolness of the silver, its weightedness. Assia traced her finger along the engraved initial. *What was Celia's last name?* **Garrett**—*was that it? Something like that,* she thought. *Irish, of course.* Assia wondered if Celia was drawn to things for their visual sense—colours, shapes—perhaps even the weight of objects in her hand. Assia set the spoon down, and turned to her laptop...

November Novel—*need to get that word count started,* she thought. Once started, the words typically flowed. It was that simple matter of getting herself started. Always, that. Assia pulled open a few more drawers, on the lookout for a corkscrew. *Ah, here we are.* Assia poured the wine, chosen for the picture on the label, into one of Celia's crystal glasses, rimmed in bronze that shone translucent in the late-afternoon light. Assia scooted the stool around to face looking outward through the long narrow window, and logged-on.

Assia's characters were in a sunnier clime now—a few of them, anyway. Some of the morose and "wordless" moods that had been extant with her characters, looked to have lifted. A couple of them were actually getting some sleep; an odd thing to note, yet the relief she felt for them struck Assia as unusual in itself.

What's been happening? The characters had scattered from one another. *And wasn't there a proposal in question?* Assia couldn't find the thread to that plot line, now.

Assia didn't want to write a novel wherein none of the characters had real-life responsibilities, such as jobs/work, to attend. These characters, though, seemed to be frequently going to work, coming from work, or taking leaves from—or thinking about finding work. And there were children involved in their lives—twins, in fact, all over the place.

Assia jumped as the phone rang into her silent reverie. She hadn't before heard the phone ring in Celia's flat. She looked at it and, after a brief moment, answered.

"Yes, Hello! I'm calling for Celia... Celia Brennan-Garrick. It's quite clear from your voice, your accent, rather—that you are not she. Is she there?"

"I... Celia is... Celia's... well, she's—not here. Assia is my name. Assia Greene. Is there something I can do for you?"

"American, I gather? Are you a flat-mate, then? Didn't know Celia had one. Andre here. A friend of hers. Jantz is the name—Andre Jantz, that is. If you would be so kind as to please tell her that Andre called, I would be ever so appreciative... s'been too long... Far too long. I'm up from Devonshire for a short while. I'll be in London for a few days—just. Hang on, I'll simply leave my cell number, if I could ask you to note it—and if I may put you to the trouble of asking Celia to ring me, when she can. Would you?"

"I'm so sorry to have to tell you this—Mr. Jantz, is it? I don't know how to say it. Celia was involved in the terrible explosion at the coffee shop near St. James Park. I'm afraid that Celia... that she... she died—in the accident."

Assia was met with a silence from Mr. Andre Jantz.

"Hello? I'm so sorry," Assia said. "Did you not know? Well, obviously... Obviously, you didn't know. I don't know what to say. Except that I'm so sorry to give you this horrific information about your friend."

There was a pause... "Good Lord... I had no idea. I... I... I'm at a loss for words. I don't know what to say. Celia..." More silence. "Who are you, then, if I may ask—a friend, I presume?"

"Actually, no—I'm a friend-of-a-friend. I'm staying here for the time being—in the flat."

"Really? Staying there... In Celia's flat?" She heard a sigh. "Celia and I were good friends. We knew one another at University, and have kept contact—albeit, sporadically—yet, I had no idea. I... I'm in shock... Wait! I must come by! I must! Yes! I need to do that... I have to see Celia's flat—once again, at the least. I know this sounds very strange. You've no idea anything about me. I'd really like to see her place once more. Have you... Well, that is to say, have you already moved everything? Painted, even—all that sort of thing?"

"No, no. I've barely begun packing things up. I've no plans to paint. I plan to leave things as they are. They're quite beautiful—unusual, actually—in a compelling way."

"Yes, yes. Quite. That's Celia's intuitive sense. Well then, I wonder how to best orchestrate this—it is quite a circumstance. I've no idea what to think—what to do. I would so very much appreciate being able to be there. I well understand the—ah—the *awkwardness*, shall we say, of this request."

This man, Andre, coming to Celia's flat? Out of the question, for Assia. An odd request, it seemed to her. Assia hardly knew what to suggest.

"Let's plan to meet first. What do you think? Perhaps, a coffee shop?" Assia said. *Oh! That was a poor choice of locations to suggest.* "Or, how about this? The Tate Gallery, since you must know where that is."

"Of course! Celia worked at the Tate, that's right. Yes, I'll meet you at the Tate," Andre said. "I'll wear something to identify myself—a green jacket, for example. Let me think one moment... Do I own a green jacket? No, I don't think I do, actually. I do not, in fact. Perhaps this, then—what do I have, here? I'll wear a long woolen scarf. Look for a man—tall, dark, and handsome— with a long woolen scarf—Caius College: pale blue, with black stripes. The scarf, that is. And let us hope there's not the lot of us sporting the same scarf whilst standing on the steps of the Tate. Shall we say noon? Saturday? I shall look for an American accent. Thus, if you could be so good as to be singing, or talking aloud to yourself, it would, of course, help ever so much... Ah, Celia! I... I am so sad. I... I lack words. All right, then, Ms. Greene, I shall see you very soon. Did we say noon? Saturday, then."

The painting was gone. Violette was stunned. How could that be? In less than a day! She talked to the Gallery owner—the man who had asked to buy the portrait from her yesterday— where she'd sat beside the Pier, lost in grief, beside the still-wet painting. The Gallery owner didn't know. "I wasn't here at the time. Must've sold first thing today—the paint could not yet be dry! It sold quite quickly! A lovely portrait, by the way. We'd be interested in more from you, if you have others for us to look at."

Violette was dismayed. She shook her head in confusion, eyebrows pulled down in thought. She'd been hasty, yesterday, in selling it. Gazing on the emergent countenance of Celia had caught her up in shock, and sadness. It had been an impulse to sell it at first offer—and so quickly. She wanted it back.

Nate carried the painting up the winding stairway of the Victorian, to Neal's apartment—curious what Neal might think of it. He slipped the loosely knotted twine from the paper that had been wrapped around the painting. He lifted the painting from the wrap, with care, and held it aloft in the light. He looked around for a place to set it, to give him a better angle on it— the right distance. *The mantle—just the place*, he thought. He moved aside a stack of books, settling the painting against the stucco walls above the broad granite-topped mantle. *This is it*, he thought... *the clearer sense of it.* Standing back a bit, Nate soaked in the *ineffable-ness*. Was that the word he needed?—the "whatever-it-was" that knew the nuances of this woman he'd loved, and had found the means to reproduce that in oils. Celia. A true beauty. Ironic, really—Celia had never seen a photo of herself that she'd liked; or, as she'd put it, one that she thought *looked the way she felt.*

Nate studied the portrait. Stillness. *Celia would've liked this*, he thought. Maybe she'd needed something softer than the sharper delineations of photos, to be comfortable with the outcome of an image of herself... something that more closely elucidated her fragile strength, her translucent beauty. Nate took in a ragged breath—there were so many ways that he found the portrait hard to look at. And harder to turn away from.

Nate decided to head downtown—hop on a bus to Neal's office, and intercept Neal on his way home. They could drive back together. He wanted to check in with the San Francisco office anyway—to see if he could take on some consulting work for them. Neal wondered if California was the better locale for him regarding trying to manage the psychological status that seemed to haunt him with what he could only describe as the *scattered agitation* sweeping through him in waves. The angle of the sun's light over the Bay was restorative for him, unlike the damp-dark chill that was London, in November. California had its November, certainly—yet the Bay's blue deepening beneath a gold-lit morning sky, was cathartic. The lifting of the fog seemed to lift something from his heart, in tandem, that was otherwise oppressive to him in ways he couldn't put words to.

Neal had already left by the time Nate arrived at his offices, having taken off a bit early to tend to his grieving houseguest. He thought it might be good for he and Nate to take the ferry—to get out on the water. Nate had never been a fan of that idea while living in the Bay area and they'd joked about it. But Nate had mentioned to Neal his obsession with the ferry; Neal thought being on the water might lift Nate's spirits. Water could be a healing force. Maybe they could take the ferry to Alcatraz on the weekend. *Maybe too bleak, altogether, given Nate's frame of mind,* Neal thought. *Or then again, it might match it. Might even help him,* in the way an external view that was strikingly similar to the internal feeling state, could provide release. He'd think about it, see what Nate thought.

Neal parked along the front curb, stepped lightly up the steps to the Victorian, and up the three flights to his apartment. Unlocking the door, he tossed his briefcase on the couch and started toward the window to open it. He wanted to let in some of the late fall air while he still had that luxury—before needing to close things up against the colder weather that would settle in, in due time.

Good God! Neal stared open-mouthed at the painting propped on the mantle. *This... this was Celia! Luminous... An angel.* Golds and violets, deep green eyes like silk. Violette had done a remarkable piece of work. Neal heard the door open behind him.

"Nate! It's... amazing! This... I can't find the words... I... I see why you fell in love with her... And I don't mean her beauty... Something else—something... *mystical* in her. Otherworldly. Okay, bad choice of words. What am I aiming for, here? *Ethereal.* That's it. The 'slightness' to her look, and then... unexpected strength running through." Neal turned toward his friend, looked at him.

"Yeah. You got it. You got her, all right," Nate said, as his voice dropped to the barest whisper.

Stephen wasn't sure he had this right. Violette had emailed to say she wanted Stephen to meet this woman, Safia—to retrieve the jeans from her and to deliver the jean to this woman, *Assia. Assia something-or-other. A colour... Assia Browne? That wasn't quite it. Was this really what she was asking?* It seemed a lot, for one thing; for another, simply bizarre. Violette seemed to think that the jeans in question belonged to this Assia person. *Assia Greene—yes, there it was, that was the name.*

Stephen had agreed to meet Safia Jumel at the Tate to procure the jeans that Violette was so concerned about. Violette had suggested the Tate as a central location, an easy place to meet a stranger. Stephen had no idea how he'd gotten so entangled in a situation Like This. He'd wondered if this could wait until Violette's return, but he was reluctant to ask her about her return.

Violette had decided she'd like to have a closer view of the Golden Gate Bridge; hop on the ferry, and glide right next to it. She wanted to feel the bridge in her skin, in her soul. It was a gorgeous Bay morning, the fog not yet burned off. She had a sudden yearning to go to Alcatraz. Odd, that desire.

Neal saw Violette approaching the line for the ferry. He recognized her right away. Of course he did. Her image was in his heart's memory. Had it only been a few years? Too long, when you've loved someone. Even if the love had been an untenable situation—which theirs had, of course, been. *What's she doing here?* He looked at her from this distance, red hair curling over her shoulders and down her back—the green raincoat that looked to be the same one she'd had when they were together back then. A favorite, he knew. That studied look of concentration he loved, as she checked something in her bag... *How had we ever gotten together? A gay man falling for a woman...* She'd broken something in him that he'd never been able to figure out. *What was it, exactly?* He'd had to pursue it, learn it, and figure it out. Which he couldn't do, and they'd both gotten hurt. They couldn't find that *comfortable and right place* to be with one another. Too much misplaced chemistry between them, and nowhere to go with it.

His emerging love for Violette had not threatened his understanding of himself a gay man. In fact, he thought the place Violette had touched in him was the same place that, so long ago, had led him to the knowing that he was gay.

Here she was, and he had no idea what to do. As when he

had first met her, his body decided for him. He had to touch her. He moved back through the line, quickly:

"Excuse me... Pardon me," he continued to say, navigating his way through the line to the spot where Violette was standing. When he got close enough to her, he reached for her arm; staring into her face, he shook his head.

"Neal," Violette reached for his hand, reflexively—looked at him. "I had no idea I'd see you. I thought I..."

She paused, looking at him. That face of his. She sighed without realizing it. That line alongside the mouth. She wanted to trace the length of it with her fingertip just as she used to, when Neal would then take her finger in his mouth and bite it, smiling at her. That smile.

"I thought about calling. I... I just got here two days ago. Still, I should have called by now. For one thing, I don't know anyone else in this city. Of course I would call you!"

Neal reached up to touch her hair, his eyes focused in unfocused thought... He stepped back, looked at Violette, and smiled the half-smile she'd come to love. "To think you're standing right in front of me," he said. "Nate's here, as well! Did you know? He's staying with me. Actually, he's with me, around here somewhere."

"Really! Well, yes, I knew he'd come. We've been in contact. He's been sending me some of his photos... I can't quite believe we're all three together... Then—you must know all about Celia. So hard—too hard, really—just all too hard, Neal. How do people manage? A loss Like This, I mean—someone they've loved so much. I haven't a clue how people do it, Neal. Do you? It's so good to look at you... You've no idea."

"Nate is quite grief-stricken—of course he is. Can hardly get any food into him at all. And then, you... Violette, I'm so sorry. Beyond managing it, for you both... Ah! I can't believe I'm seeing you! You're coming with us? Come back to my apartment, afterwards—we'll figure out dinner."

Nate looked back for Neal. *Violette!* Violette waved at him, blew him a kiss. Nate watched as Neal brushed errant strands of hair from Violette's forehead—a gesture Nate had known, himself, on occasion, from Violette.

Assia saw someone she thought might be Andre on the steps of the Tate—a dark-haired man who appeared to be looking for someone.

"Andre?"

"No. The name's Stephen, actually."

"Oh, sorry—I'm meeting someone here that I haven't met before... It's not that, whatever you're thinking. It's far more complicated than that."

"I'm sure it is," said Stephen. "I'm also meeting someone I've never met before, and it's the same—not what you might think, and rather complicated... I'm looking for a woman wearing a pale blue *hajib*."

"Ah well, I'll keep my eye out for her. And I'm looking for a man who is tall, dark, and handsome—which is why I thought perhaps you were he."

Assia caught herself. "That wasn't meant to sound the way it did. Not that that doesn't describe you, of course. What I mean to say is, that's the way the man described himself."

"I see." Stephen said. He adjusted his coat sleeve, glanced at his watch, and looked out over the walkway. "Right... This one looks like mine, though," he said to Assia, as a woman in a blue *hajib* came running up the steps to the Tate.

Aesop gathered his briefcase and notes and got into his car, parked along Jenifer Street down the block from his row house. He turned the key in the ignition. He found it odd to be dependent on a car again. He'd liked using the public transportation in London, although too often that had meant hailing a cab. Work was drudgery right now. Aesop was backlogged from his time away yet still had some wrapping up to do from his work while in London. Once he got the international work behind him, he could focus on the Native American legal briefs he was writing, work more aligned with his true passion. The excitement in the city was palpable, with the election just past.

He missed Assia, but he wasn't sure he missed London, or England for that matter. He was happy to be back in an American city, reconnecting with colleagues. He'd be meeting with a few friends for lunch today at the National Museum of the American Indian for the new exhibit: Indian/Not Indian. He'd read about it with some interest. The Museum itself was a place Aesop loved, regardless of exhibits. The structure's angled, multi-level, very public design was something Aesop appreciated. Having visited several of England's oldest museums, he'd come to renew his appreciation for the sheer spaciousness in modern architecture. The beauty of the exhibits, particularly that of the Plains Indians Exhibit—enthralled him—made him miss the Midwest and the West even more. He had a particular affection for the Midwestern city of Madison, where he'd been a student at the University of Wisconsin in the late '60s. Another highly charged time, politically—and he in the midst of it all—the students heated protests against the Viet Nam war.

"Andre Jantz?"

"And yes, there's that American accent. I saw it from a

distance. Assia! So nice to meet you." Andre held out his hand. Assia smiled, charmed, in spite of the odd circumstances of their meeting.

"Stephen? Hello." She did not reach to shake his hand. "Safia Jumel. Shall we go in then, have a quick tea? Or must you be on your way, right away?"

"Tea is fine, yes." Stephen glanced at the watch Safia was wearing on her left wrist, checked the time, and then walked with her into the museum teashop. Stephen noted that the woman who had mistaken him for someone else, was sitting with a man at a table near the doorway. *Yes, I suppose he could be described as tall and dark, and perhaps handsome.*

"Do you know them?" Safia asked.

"No, no."

Safia walked to a table by the window and hung her bag from the back of the chair.

Stephen said, "Truthfully, I do not understand this entire jeans situation."

"Nor I," Safia said. "Here, let me get them for you." She lifted her bag, reaching in for what were, apparently, the jeans in question.

Andre set the menu aside and looked at Assia. "Well, then. Let's have some lunch and catch up on old times. It seems forever. And might I say this, Ms. Assia Blue—you haven't changed at all since I last laid eyes on you. Let's take a look, shall we? It's your hair that's a bit different, then, isn't it?" Andre's light silliness made Assia laugh. She momentarily forgot her awkwardness in their being together for this first-time meeting.

"And what, might I ask, are these, exactly?" Stephen was looking at the stitching and designs and rips in the worn denim.

"Here, let me hold them up for you. One sees jeans Like This of course, but there's something about these that I particularly liked. I'm sorry to give them up, actually. Such an interesting story. Such an interesting dog! The dog must have recognized them in some way, if these are in fact the jeans your friend thinks they are. What is her name again? Violette? Unusual name. Never heard it before. Not that I am overly familiar with the usual run of British names."

Something caught Assia's attention from the corner of her eye as Andre was telling her about his friendship with Celia...

"... met Celia while we were at London University, in an art class. She studied museology. I was in the School of Architecture. We took a few classes that intersected one another's studies. We became friends, never really dated, anything like that. In fact... of course! Celia was married at the time. I forgot! Which typified the marriage and why it did not last, I think. No one knew her husband, and she did not talk about him, ever. The last few times I saw Celia were in London. She'd invited me to her flat. That's where I was first captivated by the unusual colour sense Celia liked to use, the eye she had for things. She was quite amazing. Perhaps you are seeing some... "

"HOLY SHIT! HOLY... FUCKING... SHIT!" Assia turned fully around in her chair. "This can't be... Those look like... like... Those are my jeans!"

"What?!" Andre started.

"My jeans! I can't believe what I'm seeing! I thought they'd been lost, in the... the explosion." Assia was on her feet.

184

"You are, without a doubt, one of the most unusual women I've had the pleasure of attempting to have tea with," Andre said.

Assia was at Stephen and Safia's table in a flash. She reached for the jeans. Andre was entranced. He didn't know whether it was the invocations: "Holy Shit" and "Holy Fucking Shit" or the sheer confusion of the scene that had so captured him.

"Excuse me, I—these are my jeans!" Safia's mouth was open. Assia reached for the jeans and, as Safia relinquished them, staring at her, Assia began to cry, holding them to her face. She then tucked them beneath her arm; unzipping her skirt, she began to pull it off right then and there in the Tate Gallery Museum Restaurant.

"Yes," said Andre. "Right. This Ms. Assia Greene is indeed the most interesting woman I've met for tea in quite some time. If not ever."

Andre pulled his chair forward. Stephen pushed his chair back. Stephen lifted an eyebrow and stared, a smile beginning to form, the dimple in his chin deepening. Safia turned in her chair, slightly embarrassed. Assia could not stop crying. The waitress stood poised next to Stephen's chair, pen to paper. "Perhaps I'll just stop back, then."

Violette followed Neal and Nate up the curved stairway to Neal's apartment. She remembered counting the steps on her way up to the apartment, those few years ago—sixteen steps— and that she'd been more excited to see Neal, with each step. She'd loved this apartment—set up a few levels, catching the morning sun through the floor-to-ceiling windows. She loved to watch the fog's gradual dissipation. She'd been enchanted with the old radiators that would clank and hiss as the heat came on in the early morning chill of late fall. And she remembered the gleaming hardwood floors that Neal would rub down with vinegar and water and something else that put a gorgeous sheen on the wood. "Door's unlocked, go on in," Neal called to her, stopping by the mail slot, unlocking it with a small silver key. Nate lagged behind, feeling an all-of-a-sudden wash of fatigue—momentary respite done—grief settling back into his body.

"Oh, my God!"

Nate and Neal turned to look at one another in the same moment, with the same thought—the painting...

CHAPTER XIV.

SILVER

Andre stared. He could do nothing other than. Assia was buttoning the jeans. Bending down to retrieve her skirt from the floor, she stepped back into her shoes.

Stephen could make no sense of this. *So this is Assia Greene.* He'd met her, already, on the front steps of the Tate. And now, here she was, along with Safia, who was staring at Assia and shaking her head. Assia tapped Aesop's number into her cell phone. Andre pulled his chair up to Safia and Stephen's table and introduced himself. The waitress returned. "All right then, Loves," she said. "Ready to order, then? Tea? All around?"

Aesop listened to Assia's message. *Unbelievable.* Who would've thought? He loved hearing her exclamations. *A long lost friend, these jeans.* Made Aesop wish he were there, just to see her face. He'd barely gotten back to the U.S.

Ah, missing her... *It would be ridiculous to fly back to England... Wouldn't it?*

He didn't even like to fly.

He tapped his fingers on the desktop—absent-mindedly... while an ocean away, rain pounded the windows of the Tate Gallery teashop.

When had the rain started?

Assia wasn't sure how it happened—at first she was simply offering a ride to Andre, Stephen, and Safia, it having become clear that she was the only one with a car—yet somehow, the four were in Celia's MINI, with Assia tentatively at the right-side-positioned steering wheel, all of them on their way to Celia's flat. *Is it even appropriate to call it Celia's flat any more?* Assia wondered. *It was still furnished with Celia's things—there was that.* The four pulled off their jackets and removed their shoes as they walked through the doorway of the flat, shaking the wet from their sleeves. *Now what?*

Violette snugged her green jacket close to her body, and

stepped off Pier 13 onto the ferry. The fog-burning morning light on the bay was a startling teal-blue—*"Bright enough to curl your hair," as Grandmother Fiona would've said*, Violette thought. It was, though, always a bit chilly on the water; Violette was glad she'd remembered the chilly Bay air, and that she'd run back to retrieve her jacket this morning when she'd left.

Violette stood close to Nate, close, yet not touching. The ferry pulled out into San Francisco Bay and Nate tipped his head to the wide-open sky. "Doesn't seem England has skies Like This," Violette said. "That blue... I wonder if I could conjure that for the background to the Golden Gate. I'll need many colours to achieve it: greens, deep purples, blues... gold. I'll need to go back to Paint or Dye."

"Paint or... dye? Never heard of it," said Neal.

Violette shaded her eyes against the sun, catching the sign: ALCATRAZ AND ANGEL ISLAND. That juxtaposition—

Angel... Alcatraz. Alcatraz had been a prison for much of its history, Violette knew. But she wasn't sure what else Alcatraz had been. A lighthouse, she thought—not even sure how she knew that. A military base of some sort? Violette remembered having seen *The Bird Man of Alcatraz*, as a child, and tried to recall any spurious thing she knew of Alcatraz—couldn't come up with much. She thought Alcatraz meant

pelican and wondered if there were still pelicans on the island.

She recalled unconnected bits of information—that the first men to be imprisoned on Alcatraz were American Civil War conscientious objectors, and that Alcatraz had been closed down as late as the 1960s. Perhaps she could find information—brochures—when on the island. Nate was already photographing it, as they neared sight.

Violette soaked in the subtlety of colours among the ruins and decaying architecture: the partial brick walls, empty windows opened to the sea and sky... corroded buildings. A brick fireplace, in nearly perfect shape, stood against the shell of a small rectangular shape. *A prison cell,* Violette supposed. Errant green shrubs and grasses grew thick where floors had been. Red blooms and wildly thick flora stood choir-like in the decomposition. Hovels, paint-faded to the merest evidence of a faded slate colour, stood stalwartly amidst crumbling structures grayed by wind, salt, air, sun, time. The modest decaying structures crouched beneath V-shaped, angled rooftops, stepped against one another in varying heights. White birds—pelicans?—perched on the rusted tin roofs and chimney tops. She wondered what it would have been like to be imprisoned on this island, looking at sea and sky running out farther than the eye could see—or gazing across the Bay, watching the fog open its curtains on the glittering city that was San Francisco.

Even more than Alcatraz, the return trip to San Francisco drew Nate's photographer's eye. The water—gunmetal, blue-gray-green. Sun pouring viscous wide-swathed light onto the surface of the bay, watercolor wash running luminous blue right up to the dock at Pier 13. *Wonder what Celie would come up with, for a name for that colour?* He tried breathing the light into skin, bones, heart and soul.

Nate's photos captured the blues amidst wild gold light—photos that Violette would later frame and place on the walls of her apartment—an apartment she didn't yet own, and could not yet envision at the moment those pictures were being taken.

Assia thought she should make coffee for everyone, since they were all a bit wet, but she could only find the electric teakettle, which she didn't know how to use—*couldn't be all that hard, could it?*

"Here, love," said Andre and Safia, together. "I'll do it."

Stephen wandered Celia's flat. "Odd that I've never been here," he said. "They were best friends, you know—Celia and Violette—well I suppose you must know that now. I saw Celia quite often—with Violette—yet I'd not been to her flat. I see her—Celia—in these details—this collection on her desk, for example—these colours... Celia had a sense of... well, what would one call it, truly?" He shrugged. "An unusual sense, of whatever it is—'style' doesn't seem quite the word for it. Violette often made mention of that. Celia did amazing displays at the Tate—that I do know. I'm sorry you didn't have the opportunity to meet her." Assia nodded, watching Stephen, as his eyes swept the room slowly, taking it all in.

"Whatever will you do with all of her things?" he said. "Pity, there's no family—such as it is, that is to say—interested in her belongings. I expect that no one really knew her as intimately as Violette had. Perhaps that fellow Celia saw... Nate. Has to be tough for him, as well. I can only imagine... So much has happened in only a few weeks. Feels much longer than that, doesn't it? Hard to think that Violette's in California now—seems so far away. Well, it is, actually—far, that is. She missed California, I know... In part, I have to wonder if she'll return. I haven't wanted to say that aloud."

"Stephen, have you been there... to California?" Assia asked.

"Yes, actually, I have. I taught for a semester at Pomona College in Claremont. Great part of the U.S. So completely 'other' than London—or Oxford, certainly. Or even the East Coast

Universities in the States. I can understand Violette's liking it as much as she does. I remember her comments about the light, in the Bay area—that it's very different than the light in London, for painting outside, you know—as is her preference. She much preferred that light."

Stephen paused, his eyes on a print of Celia's, leaning against the wall. "Fancy this. What do you make of it?"

The print had been placed on the hardwood floor beneath a row of windows, leaning against the pale blue wall—as if Celia had yet to find the *comfortable and right* place for it. Assia moved closer to catch the fine print beneath the print: Joseph Albers: *Departing in Yellow 1964.*

"I'm familiar with this artist," Assia said. "I've always rather liked him, which is a bit odd, in fact—in that typically I'm not drawn to art of this period. I like this series of geometrics and colours he's done—the four squares of this print—well, that's how I see it, at least—squares—departing into the deep bright yellow at the center... You don't care for it?"

"Oh no, nothing like that. Seems a bit out of place in this room. Can't say why."

"Hmmm... Yes, I see what you mean—Perhaps it's the colours... they seem *off* in relation to the wall and ceiling colours of this room—this pale blue, and the adjacent red-orange—the turquoises, that glossy green trim on the windows. I'd have to say my favorite is the ceiling—pale aqua blue. Blue like... like a lullaby—that's the best I can come up with for it—for how I feel standing beneath it Like This... There's something about being in this room that *settles me*," Assia said. *What was it, exactly?* — The ease in the arrangement of the furniture, for example... that there seemed to be no set rules that were followed and yet the room was not chaotic, in sensibility—was soothing, instead. She looked at Stephen who was now holding the print in his hands. "I wonder," he said. "Perhaps the print had special meaning for her."

Assia sat on Celia's couch, while Stephen perused the room.

She leaned back, lost in her own thoughts. Andre and Safia were still in the kitchen, readying the tea. For days now, Assia had felt the grip of her deep loneliness abating—the abyss that she could usually count on to knock the breath out of her. When she and Aesop had first arrived in England and she'd had no structure to her days, there seemed to be no barrier to, at all. She recalled walking along the Thames the day they'd met Violette, feeling raw-sweeping loneliness soak into her skin like the damp chill English air. Her loneliness for Aesop was different, a longing that felt okay, in its own way, to Assia—manageable.

Andre and Safia returned from the kitchen, Andre balancing the large tray—teapot, tea cups, a silver service sugar bowl and an empty creamer—all, stacked amidst cloth napkins, a tangle of silver spoons—and an ornately labeled box. *Must be sugar cubes,* Assia decided.

"There was no milk that was anywhere near fresh," said Andre. "We must go through the Frigidaire and simply toss everything. Sad, this business... Ah, no words for it, are there? I'm at a loss. Full-out and utter loss for words. If I pause at all, to think of something, anything—to say about this... this horror, really—then there's too much sadness to fend off. Too much abrupt shock of loss. How does one manage this? How is it possible? I ask you that." Andre settled the tray on Celia's desk, carefully pushing a stack of papers to the side; he then sat on the couch, next to Assia.

"Assia—do you see what I mean, then?—why I had to come back here to see Celia's work—her *touch*? Never a white ceiling, wherever Celia made 'home' for herself. Even her student lodgings absorbed her creativity, like a sponge.

"The beautiful seduction of unusual colour. Much like Celia herself," said Andre. "She had a quality of drawing one in, towards her. Celia's intricacies... the silver bracelets she wore—each day—never saw her without them; the nail polish she loved... what was the colour name—the deep indigo polish she liked? She told me the name, once; I thought I'd never forget. Something... "

Assia, Stephen, Andre, and Safia, who had met one another only a few hours previous, sat in Celia's flat in London—rain spattering the leaves of the Black Maple Tree in the courtyard below—drinking tea they'd found in Celia's cupboard—Into the Mystic tea. "Ah, yes," said Andre, "Celia must have chosen this tea for the name. It would be just like her."

"Stephen, could I pour some tea for you?" Assia asked, holding a cup at the ready.

"Lovely sugar, this," Safia said, shaking the intricately coloured box to release several brown sugar cubes.

"*Ink!*" Andre exclaimed. "That's it! -the nail polish Celia favored..."

It wasn't, in fact, the name of the tea motivating Celia's purchase; she'd chosen the tea for the blue colour of the tea tin. She'd found the flavor of the tea quite distateful, actually, but as that hadn't been the reason for her purchase she didn't much mind. She'd matched the blue of the tea tin for the windowed wall in the living room—the wall where her print *Departing in Yellow* now leaned, awaiting its *comfortable and right place*, wherever that might be. Her guests, drinking their tea with sugar, and without milk, had no idea.

"—Yes, that was it—*Ink*—because she loved to write, she told me—and it reminded her of inkwells! Or some such thing that I can't quite fully recall—although that sounds quite right, don't you think? That's the way Celia made decisions—no discernible logic. And yet, a logic of her own sort, all the same."

Nate, Neal, and Violette sat on the deeply velvet couch in Neal's San Francisco apartment, drinking a Malbec wine, which a friend had brought Neal from South America—while only Nate knew that Celia had written Malbec wine into her November Novel—the wine, *still as prayer*—while her character had tried very hard not to fall in love with a man she could not have. And on the mantle, Violette's portrait of Celia, that Nate had bought— awaited its *comfortable and right place,* wherever that might be.

Chaucer shook the rain from his fur and circled in his favorite spot next to the gas fireplace in the home of the Millieners-de la Pontes,

...while Jean-Oscar shook off his wet rain jacket and prepared to make tea.

...while Aesop got out of his car and hurried up the steps to his row house on this street—"Jenifer" Street—in Washington D.C., rain spattering the sidewalk in what appeared to be prelude for much more to come—he unlocked the door, tossed his briefcase onto the nearby couch, and went into the kitchen where he poured himself a glass of Napa Valley wine. Holding the glass to the light, he paused, gazing deeply—the wine, deeply red—was shot through with rich amber light—*Very still, this wine. Like velvet.*

Andre invited the others to have some of this most patiently awaited tea. "Assia, tell us what you're doing here. Not that I know what any of us are doing here in London, including myself, actually—but let's at least start with you—since you are obviously from furthest away, and since you're our host—even though you didn't have so much as a clue how to find your way 'round the kitchen, or serve the tea, even. We forgive you that."

Assia furrowed her brows, thinking... "Well, yes—I am—or rather, last I left off, I was... I might be... well that is... living here—London, that is—but then again, I may be going back to D.C. It's a bit confusing, now that I think of putting words to it. Yet, I'm giving thought to staying here. I mean to say, *right here*—in Celia's flat, actually." The three guests looked up all together, wordless.

"Staying on, you mean to say?" Safia said, "As in... well, for months? Indefinitely, that is?"

"I hadn't thought too awfully much beyond the present several weeks, if I had to say," said Assia.

"You do seem a bit unsure, what with all the 'might be,' 'may be,' 'last left off,' 'thinking ofs,'" Andre said, "Yet, your being here, in the flat—has a certain soothing-ness to it, even though you hadn't known Celia. Rather an interesting idea, actually."

"Yes... well... and what about you, Safia?" Assia said.

"Perhaps I'm a bit less confused than are you." Safia started laughing again. This Assia made her laugh quite a bit, though the situations they found themselves in together were not necessarily funny.

"My lodgings are near Kensington Gardens, at present. I am hoping to move closer to the University. My main interest, passion I suppose one would call it, is acting. I'm involved with a play right now, in fact—at the theatre off Market Street. Are you acquainted with the theatre?"

Stephen nodded. "Yes, of course! Then you're an actress?"

"Of sorts, yes. One cannot make a living at it though, or should I say that I certainly couldn't. I am currently teaching at the University of London—the drama department—as well as acting."

"Ah, yes!" said Stephen. "You know, I've been thinking that I've actually crossed paths with you, somewhere. Perhaps it was there. I teach in the physics department, although I've been in Oxford this term... Not that there's a lot of crossover between drama and physics—other than metaphysically, of course, now that I put my mind to it."

Safia smiled.

"You do seem somewhat familiar to me," Stephen said. "Cannot fathom why."

"Nor can I," said Safia. "I rarely venture from things dramatic. Perhaps you have seen a play that I was in?"

Stephen had to think. He was not much for plays, concerts, and those sorts of things that Violette had always been trying to get him to, yet they'd seen something at Market Theatre last year.

What had it been? They'd gone just before Violette had married Simon, one of the last times he and Violette had been together.

Andre poured more tea. "This is actually rather... well, *enigmatic* tea," he said. "Not altogether pleasant-tasting, frankly. The scent calls to mind something that I can't seem to put my finger on..."

"Ah! The Shakespeare play!" said Stephen, turning to Safia. "The one with the twins! That's where I saw you! Violette—the woman I was seeing, Celia's best friend, Celia of this flat—had wanted to see it. Violette has twins, you know—and she'd wanted Celia and Nate to join us, because Nate has twins, as well. Well, of course, that was not the only motivation to attend the play, but there was a synchronicity that appealed to her, as I recall."

"*As You Like It*," Safia said. "I did have a part in that play. Amazing that you even put that together. I hope to do another Shakespeare play, actually, upcoming in the spring. I plan to audition for the role of Mistress Ford in *The Merry Wives of Windsor*. It's a role I've played once before, in Stratford, and would welcome the opportunity to take it on in this venue."

"Ah yes!" Andre said, "The play where Falstaff utters the line: 'Let the sky rain potatoes! Let it thunder to the tune of 'Greensleeves'! Celia and I saw *The Merry Wives of Windsor* while at University together. She'd fixated on that line; had me, later, look it up for her. She'd always loved 'Greensleeves'— the music, and the painting. Dante Rossetti's *Greensleeves*. She used to have a reproduction of it... Can't quite recall how Greensleeves actually fit in to the play, or if it was one of those mysteries that pop into Shakespearian plays. Well, a mystery to the lay observer, let me just say that. I remember thinking it a bit off, that—Celia's love for the so-haunting *Greensleeves*; Celia always felt she walked a too-close line, as it was, to what she referred to as... What was it now?... that word she used... angst—that's it—the feeling of nameless sorrow."

"One of my favorites, as well—*Greensleeves*—I do not recall the line, though—that of Falstaff. Now you've got me curious. I shall need to go back and take a look at the script," Safia said, setting her tea aside. *Something odd about the taste of this tea—* she thought, eyes drawn to the painting propped against the wall in the entryway... *Looks like a river...* she thought, *or a larger body of water, perhaps... Hard to say...*

Andre paused. "Here's something odd for you... I've come to London to talk with an architectural firm about a project they're taking on, of just the sort that I like to lend myself to and become immersed in. I'm an architect—perhaps I've not said? I think I told you that, Assia, when we first talked. Perhaps not, though. Ah, no matter... The project is, ironically, to rebuild the coffee shop—the one that met with the unfortunate accident— St. James Park... the, ah... explosion. Horrific to even use that word, especially right here in Celia's flat." He sighed.

"Although, I think it's a good thing if I can work in this capacity, for Celia's sake, in some way that I cannot even begin to find words for." The others looked up, all together, speechless, and stared at him. Assia spoke first:

"Really? That's... that is... I think it's actually... good, perhaps—as you say."

"The owner wants to rebuild. It's to be expanded in size, somewhat. Space is wanted for near to seventy tables. She's requested outlets at most of those tables. I assured her that computers would have less need for outlets, and soon, but she was insistent—said she needed them for the coffeepots. Couldn't fathom what she meant... She's even chosen a new name for it: 'November Novel Coffee Shop.' I can't say I know what that means, either. She wants to dedicate the month of November to patrons who work on this 'November Novel' phenomenon. They would be the only customers allowed during the entire month of November. Novel idea. Pun, intended."

Assia smiled. "Of course! What a tribute! Very creative. Seems healing, in a way. I'm working on the November Novel myself... Or I certainly should be. I haven't done my words for today! I have no idea what my word count is, actually," she said, brows drawing downward, calculating word-count possibilities in her mind. The others looked at her, confused.

CHAPTER XV.

RAIN

Neal perched on the stool at his kitchen counter, tapping pen on paper, planning Thanksgiving dinner. He'd insisted to Violette and Nate that they be there, and both had accepted his invitation. Nate had seen no reason to return to England, yet. This was not a holiday wherein his presence would be missed. He'd need to figure out Christmas, of course—and soon. Would he be ready to go back? Should he think about bringing his family over here? He didn't think Lauren would want to fly to California. The twins were too young to do so on their own, even as "unaccompanied minors," and he didn't like the thought of that—the flight was too long.

Violette disliked most holidays. She didn't understand Thanksgiving, even though it had been explained to her. She didn't like the colours and hype of holidays, particularly in America. Everywhere she went, no matter what holiday was approaching—and in the States it seemed there was always a holiday approaching—colours jumped out at her, nearly aggressively, she thought; garish, out of context, out of place, decorations that disturbed her senses. Too much of everything.

Violette had been at Neal's the Thanksgiving she'd been in California three years ago—where she'd first met Nate—showing her that a holiday centered on Neal's home cooking was, indeed, manageable. More than manageable... Delightful. Neal tended to take in all manner of people for holiday celebrations, those far from family, for example—making for great interest, and indeed, a *charm*, as well.

Aesop had to figure out what to do for Thanksgiving now that he was back in the States. He'd been invited to several homes, as people knew that for all intents and purposes he'd be "alone" for the holiday. Yet, he wanted to stay in, and work. He wouldn't be permitted to, he was sure. Thanksgiving held too much import for people; most could not bear the thought of anyone being alone on the occasion. Oh, for Assia to be here. Workdays kept him more than busy, but non-structured times like holidays held him hostage. Assia had felt the same, regarding her "blues." She said an angst could wind through her, like a damp fog—could infiltrate the tiniest opening in her day. Still, she managed—somehow—and very well. She used to say that she was one of the "high-functioning depressed," making it hard for her to be taken seriously when complaining of feeling really low. He had had to admit seeing Assia change in the weeks they'd been in England, though he wasn't sure why. Perhaps in that regard alone, it was good that she'd stayed on. *But for a full year?* That was too long for Aesop.

Assia intended to write on what would be Thanksgiving Day in the U.S. No one she knew here, in London, would expect her to either make dinner or attend someone else's. She was way behind on word count as it was, and wanted a long day to catch up. Now that her unexpected guests had (reluctantly) left, she thought she'd try to write for the two-or-more hours usually needed, to get in the daily amount of words. The unusualness of the day had carried into evening. It had felt good to have people in the flat—making tea, talking, looking, wandering, asking questions—laughing even. It was probably very good for Celia's flat to be filled with life and energy—new relationships linking.

She tried to remember where she'd left off. She remembered she hadn't been able to make sense of things, as per usual, with her characters' comings and goings. She'd tracked her characters to the United States—someplace warm and sunny. Some had begun finding one another. The mood of malaise that various characters had been harboring, had waned. New energy had entered in the form of a few new characters, but she wasn't sure what they were about. She didn't understand what had happened to the supposed engagement of two characters. But perhaps that was merely her interpretation of the word *proposal*, which could mean other things besides an engagement. She logged on.

Ah, what's this? Assia was havixg trouble with her keyboard all of a suddex. Her "n" key would xo loxger prixt. The key had mutixied. She had to figure out what to do, to contixue to be able to write today. Substitutixg ax "x" would have to do—it was goixg to slow her dowx, defixitely. Maxy words behixd ox "couxt" already, this was throwixg her. Xothixg to be doxe about it toxight. She'd try to get axother keyboard that she could adapt to her laptop, ix the morxixg. Assia sat back ix her chair. There was somethixg dramatic goixg ox ix the xovel. She wasx't sure what. She decided to stop for the xight. She'd try to catch up tomorrow, whex she hoped to get her keyboard situatiox resolved, axd type with catching-up speed.

Neal brainstormed, for his Thanksgiving dinner plans.

Safia attended the evening rehearsal *All That is Gold*, based on Tolkien's Trilogy.

Andre sketched plans for: November Novel Coffee Shop.

Nate and Violette stepped onto the ferry, planning that Nate shoot some night photos of the bridge.

Assia immersed herself in *November Novel*.

She was relieved that her free-floating anxiety about a portended dramatic situation did not seem to be extant, anywhere. None of her characters seemed in imminent danger. She sat back in her chair, wondering if she should try to figure out if she could possibly get coffee going... Yet, her novel beckoned. All of a sudden a chill swept through Assia. She'd let go her anxiety too soon. One of the characters... male, someone on his own in the novel at present, seemed to be heading for something... seemed it was an accident about to happen—she didn't know what, though. She sat as still as she could.

Assia stopped. She didn't want to write it—whatever it was. She was still distressed over losing one of her favorite main characters, one that had died in a disaster in what turned out to be an early chapter of this November Novel. Assia didn't think the novel could take another loss like that. She knew she couldn't.

Perhaps he was headed for only a minor mishap. It didn't feel that way. Her apprehensions were too large. She didn't want to find out... seemed there was a river involved. Were any of her characters near one?

Coffee. That's what I need. I'll just step away from this; I'll try again, in a bit.

Aesop, having decided to meet friends for a late dinner, turned the ignition in his car. The rain that had started earlier in the evening was now turning to sleet in the near-freezing temperature—sticking to the windshield. *Cold for Washington D.C.—rarely see snow in November... streets will be slippery.* He turned on the windshield wipers while pulling onto Connecticut Avenue, taking a quick sideways glance to the front windows of one of his favorite bookstores, Politics and Prose, which is where he saw it:

NOVEMBER NOVEL, BY ASSIA GREENE

The front window. He startled. Then decided, as he continued onward—negotiating the sleet and the cars in front of him—that what he must have seen was the bookstore's advertisement for "November Novel Month."

I miss her—that's all. That's what this is... missed her so much he could see her name right in front of his eyes. Aesop turned off Connecticut Avenue, deciding to take the 14th Street Bridge across the Potomac.

Assia was afraid to continue writing. She didn't have it in her to face anything happening to one of her characters, not after the day she'd had. She tapped her fingers on the edge of the desk, stalling her writing. *I'll call Aesop... It would be, hmmm... around 1:00 a.m. if I have that figured right... I'll have to wait. I'll try calling around noon, London time, and catch him before he leaves for work... see if he's gotten the message I left about the jeans.* She looked down at them, ran her fingers over the peace sign embroidered in purple thread. *How could it be that I've never noticed this peace sign before? After all the times I've worn these jeans...* She put her fingers through the tear in the jeans where Aesop had put his, the day she'd met Violette and had been captivated with Violette's painting of the Golden Gate Bridge.

Assia tried to finally leave off the novel for a bit, but was distracted by another sort of words streaming... insistent. The words seemed to be taking the form of a poem in several stanzas. In the midst of her novel?! *What's this?* Assia watched the words wind down the page, while she typed them.

HOLDING ON

I.

Eight years of age—boy and girl.
Their trust in one another locks their hearts.
Light brown hair,
*   tangling over her shoulders.*
Leather band binding his ink-dark ponytail, trailing down his back.

II.

Bright eyes, she—his eyes, dark, into night-sky blue.

They're in deep water together... brown muddy moving water.

They hold one another's arms,

    her fingers around his forearm, his around hers.

Across the wreckage of something they've found floating in the
water. Or perhaps it found them.

III.

Is it a log... floating? Or a branch from a tree— securing them?

Her dress... is pale yellow, sun-faded, worn leather.

    marked with red crisscrosses, scattered with tiny beads:

    green, violet, gold, turquoise.

Fringe zigzags the length of his long leather pants,

IV.

Moccasins kicked off on the shoreline,

    two pair, loose in the sand,

    absorbing the heat of noontime sun.

She's smiling—laughing at their play.

They have a history of play together.

V.

Are they in danger?

There's no one around.

Except wildlife in the woods. And butterflies.

And dragonflies,

    buzzing in the heat.

VI.

Is this a flood? Or is this the river they swim and play in?

And they've just gotten in too deep...

Is there a danger of one of them letting go?

If one lets go, what will happen?

Their arms would never get tired—

Would they?

VII.

She tilts her head, looks up, closing her eyes, briefly, against the sun's bright

light, then levels a steady look at him. "I've always been a good swimmer.

If one of us has to let go, we'll swim for the shore. We'll find our way...

Apart for a time, maybe—meeting up with one another again, just—

Like This."

VIII.

"I'm happy that we met (again)— in this lifetime we're in."

She turns, eyes following the arc of a dragonfly.

"I need to tell you this," she says, "—the most important thing... "

But she doesn't say it, because he's saying something to her, and she's laughing.

The sun bounces over her eyelashes, as she looks at him,

meeting his gaze straight on.

Assia gazed at the stanzas trying to make sense of them in the context of her novel. The cell phone rang out, loudly. Assia jumped. Where was it? Assia followed the insistent jangling to the depths of the couch cushions—answered it.

"Assia, it's Stephen. About Chaucer. I need to tell Violette.

Not sure what to do. I thought I would run it by you. I was hoping Chaucer would turn up rather quickly, and that I could, thereby, avoid alarming Violette. What is she going to be able to do from California, anyway—except worry?"

Assia didn't know how to advise Stephen, and now her worry for Aesop had taken her mind's focus. She told Stephen to wait through the night, England time, and see what happened tomorrow. Aesop interrupted Stephen's call.

Neal tabulated how many to expect for dinner: Nate, Violette, and himself, plus four interns from his firm: "Thanksgiving orphans." He remembered Violette's objection to the term—such a cavalier use of the word "orphan," she'd said... Nate tapped his pen on the counter, thinking. No doubt, several other friends would join them. Twelve? He'd plan on that number and get things together as quickly as possible. The month had sped up on him. *Thanksgiving, tomorrow! How could that be?!*

Nate adjusted the lens on his Nikon. The dark was turning to an eerie airlessness. Clouds roiled, rain imminent. Violette pulled up the hood of her jacket and moved to stand next to Nate. Waiting. She thought about the un-likeliness of it all— standing next to Nate on the ferry—here in San Francisco, and just weeks after Celia's death. Celia, whom they had each loved, distinctly—each, as deeply. Violette buttoned her green jacket all the way up, scanning the dark San Francisco Bay, its deepening blues bleeding seamlessly into the sky. The ferry had made a wide-arced turn, and was heading back. Nate leaned out and over the railing, positioning himself for a shot of the lights reflecting from the bridge. Violette reflexively reached to hold him *steady*, threading her fingers through the back belt loops of his jeans, holding on.

"Thanks, Violette, I'm okay."

Violette smiled. That *okay* word that she loved. Never sounded right when she tried to say it. Nate got the shots he wanted, stepped back from the railing and turned, circling his arms around Violette, drawing her essence close in.

"I'm so fucking sorry for us both... so sorry," he said. "I know how much she meant to you." Violette sighed into his jacket, her face wet with rain and tears. *Will I ever stop crying?* She wanted to be back, already, next to the fireplace in Neal's apartment. She felt cold all the way into her bones. She didn't think she'd be warm enough, again. Violette looked at Nate, the glow from blinking foghorn lights barely illuminating his eyes. "Nate, Celia loved you... You know that... I know you do," she said, putting her hand over his heart. "Right there," she said.

Aesop's cell phone was ringing. Assia. He negotiated traffic. The car behind him had been practically on his bumper since he'd hit the main road toward the bridge.

"Aesop!"

"Assia, I'm driving. Let me try to pull over. There's a guy behind me in some kind of hurry."

Aesop looked for an opening to exit to the side of the road just as the bridge over the river came nearly into reach. The car behind him swerved past, picking up speed—and while Aesop turned his attention to Assia's voice, his eyes followed the taillights zigzagging raggedly as the car hit black ice, swerved, skidded into the guard rail, and broke through. Aesop, stunned, could barely register Assia's alarmed voice.

"Aesop, it's Chaucer! Violette's dog. He's missing! I hope to God he hasn't been hit by a car. I've had awful premonitions about a car accident all evening."

Neal was looking for the bottle of Indonesian vanilla he'd found at the market on Geary Street. He absolutely needed it for his Chocolate-Bourbon-Pumpkin Pie recipe—one of a kind—his great-grandfather's. Neal freely gave the recipe out to anyone who requested it, and many did. But it required so many ingredients that few actually attempted making it. Neal didn't really make anything the same way twice. Recipes were simply a leaping-off point, something to set on the counter while he experimented. Neal was so often distracted by tangential ideas when he cooked, that, at times, he found it hard to get *whatever-it-was* into the oven.

Neal pounded the wooden handle of a large whisk into an angulated chunk of organic, dark Madagascar chocolate, gathering up the splintered hunks of chocolate scattered over the counter. Madagascar chocolate could be found only on Powell Street, as far as he knew. He retrieved the glass bottle of maple syrup from the cupboard, the best maple syrup was from Vermont or Canada, in Neal's experience. His bottle was getting low—might have to track down more for the recipe. Bourbon, next, followed with butterscotch and lemon-flavored Jell-Os as a *chaser*—ingredients Neal thought of in the category of the *ridiculous*, yet, brought an important, albeit nearly indiscernible flavor.

He wondered how things were on the ferry. The weather portended rain. Not sure how it was on the Bay. Though, night-time on the Bay ferry was often magical, regardless of weather.

Neal wandered into the living room, solely to look at the painting again. It brought him up close—close to what, he couldn't say. Couldn't articulate that. He'd find himself stopping in front of the painting whenever he walked through the room, that being many times per day, centered as the room was between the kitchen and the other spaces of the apartment. He wondered what would become of this painting of the beloved Celia. Neal was sure that Nate intended to keep it—but just exactly *where*, he had no idea. He didn't know if Nate would actually take him up on the offer to keep it here. *And Violette... What would she do next? Tough situation for those two... all of it. Very, very tough. He hardly knew what to say to either of these friends whom he loved so much—Nate and Violette.*

He gathered that Violette had left her marriage. Her youngest two, twins, would be off for University in the fall. He hadn't met the girls, though he'd met Eli—Violette's son. Eli had worked in one of Neal's bakeries for him, the summer after his sophomore year of college. Very cool kid—completely taken with the sourdough breads of San Francisco; couldn't get enough of them—had an almost intuitive sense for baking that had surprised Violette. She'd no idea where that talent had come from. Neal understood Eli's passion for the nuances of baking bread. He'd spent many afternoons with Eli, showing him intricacies of technique that produced the bread that had made Neal's bakery a favorite in the city. Neal didn't know what Eli may eventually do with this particular talent—bread-making— among the many talents that were emergent in the young man he was becoming. Eli had wide-ranging interests already. He was enraptured with India, having twice traveled to that country to study with the monks. That much Neal remembered. That much was all he could handle remembering. No one had expected Eli's disappearance. How could they have, no matter their worries about this nomadic wandering-one? None who knew and loved Eli had any idea, any idea at all, how to navigate life with this unknown, how to hold onto faith. And hope. Possibility. Love for

Eli had brought Neal to *praying*. Something he had until then, missed, in his life.

Violette used to talk about moving to California. He wondered how she felt about that idea now. She could certainly make some kind of living with her painting; he knew that, now, in looking at this portrait of Celia, if he hadn't known it before when he'd been so moved with her art. His eyes moved over the golds, the pale colors that countenanced this *angel* on his mantle. He'd never met Celia. A regret he hadn't known, till now, that he'd carried. He would like to have known the woman his best friend had loved, the best friend of the woman he had loved. The *tangled web*. String theory. *Hidden extra dimensions.* He was a novice, when it came to physics, yet liked reading about it, making the metaphoric leap to relationships among people. The world *snapping into different configurations*. String theory seemed to answer questions for Neal that he couldn't figure out how to ask; the answers, though only partially comprehensible to him, brought him to a certain place, within—*a comfortable and right place*. Maybe Eli was in there, in *that* place, wherever it was. Why did he so strongly feel he would yet lay eyes on that child, again? He could feel Eli in his heart, skin, and soul. It was the very *knowing* he held to, strongly, that the prayers had threaded in-and-through him, containing all things: grief, fear, love, and hope. Faith.

Neal decided to get a fire going in the fireplace. It might be a long evening. Nate and Violette would be cold when they got back.

"Hold up, Assia. There's been an accident right in front of me. I'm going to call you back after I get out of the way. I hear sirens, already. I'll call you." The line went silent.

"Aesop!" Fear crept through Assia's stomach like an ominous tide. She'd had premonition dangling, all evening. She waited impatiently for Aesop to call back. In the meantime, she completely forgot Chaucer's plight. She wandered the flat, thought to make tea—for once—then decided against dealing with the electric teakettle. *How complicated could it be? Wouldn't a person just plug it in?* She tapped her fingers on the counter—opened the refrigerator. Still no food. Andre had cleared everything out for her. The phone rang.

"Yes... Aesop?!"

"Assia, I'm fine. I've no idea what happened to the driver; how could he have survived?! I can hardly let my mind go there... I'm turning around, heading back home—need to calm myself down. I'm actually shaking. Can't get that image out of my mind—the lights, the car breaking through the guardrails..." There was a pause. "... Assh, I'm sorry about Chaucer... will have to get back to you tomorrow." An emotion of another kind swept through Aesop: "Come back, Assia, back to D.C. I'm tired of living separately. I miss you."

"Aesop, I'm so relieved you're all right. You have no idea how that scared me! E., we'll talk tomorrow—after you've slept. If you're too upset to sleep tonight, call me. I'll be here."

Assia reached for Celia's green silk robe, slipped into it... Worrying about Aesop Like This... She needed to relax. Maybe she'd see if she could figure out the teakettle, after all, and sit down for a moment with a cup of hot tea.

Jean-Oscar was beside himself. He could not fathom where Chaucer had gotten to! Somehow, the dog must've gotten out of the house when the door was ajar. Jean-Oscar could not imagine how, nor where, Chaucer would've gone. He'd dashed out to the main road, the most likely place for a dog to run, fearing he would find an injured Chaucer—the heavy traffic on the road being Jean-Oscar's worst present-moment fear. He would not forgive himself if anything happened to the dog. Simply would not. Ever. This, he knew. Elodie and Claude had called a taxi service, and were traversing the main roads up and back, and then up again, searching. The police had been alerted, though they could do very little. The Animal Control service had no leads.

Violette and Nate drove back through the valley into San Francisco. Violette decided she couldn't face her hotel room. "I'll come with you to Neal's for the night. I'm sure he'll put me up on the couch. Or knowing Neal, insist on my taking a bed." Nate knew hotel life too well, and thought Violette's staying at Neal's, a good plan. The damp of the steady drizzle permeated every layer they'd been wearing, even their rain jackets. They were both soaked through to a bone-dampening, misted chill. Nate had some nice shots of the bridge—or at least he hoped he had. He recalled the excerpt of Celia's November Novel she'd sent him via the email—the detail of having her characters meet on the ferry, thinking it was romantic. The too-familiar ache of missing her overtook him. He indulged himself, for once letting the actual words come to mind—*I wish. I wish Celie were right here.* He remembered the words that comforted him: *Allow yourself to want things, no matter the risk in trying. Desire is never the mistake.* Would that he could have shown Celia the Bay area of California that he loved so much. Maybe it was time to move back here. Maybe.

Aesop was in near shock. He arrived home without knowing

how he'd gotten there. He had the presence of mind to check-in with his friends, waiting at the restaurant for him. He obsessively replayed the image of the car accelerating past him, hitting the ice. It could have been him. He didn't want his thoughts to go down that trail. All of a sudden Aesop was not sure what to do. Assia. Could they handle a year apart?

Neal opened the door to his two rain-bedraggled friends, and made them sit by the fireplace while he warmed drinks for them. "I've got to figure out where to get some maple syrup—I drained the bottle... need the right kind... " He grabbed his rain jacket from the closet and pulled it on, snapping the cuffs over his wrists to keep out the damp air. "... going over to Geary St. to see what I can come up with it. Get yourselves warmed up and let's load those photos on the computer, when I get back I want to see what you got on a rainy night Like This."

"Jeez, I hope something, man, for all the miserable wet we were in," Nate said. "The light was something—or rather the 'no light.' Just the bridge illumination. Magical. I'm curious what I might have been able to photograph of it."

Assia picked up *Canterbury Tales* from Celia's beside table, tucking herself into Celia's bed under the gold duvet, fluffed-to-floating, just the way Celia had liked it.

Violette fell asleep in front the fire on Neal's couch of deepest velvet green, the gold silk comforter that Neal had tucked in around her, floating her into blessedly dreamless sleep.

Aesop poured a glass of wine, light floating crystal reflections, turning the wine to pale gold.

Neal, having returned with the coveted maple syrup, after all, pulled up a chair next to Nate as both intentfully focused on the computer screen; Nate's photos of the Golden Gate Bridge, taken from the ferry, floated into view, locking their gazes: the bridge, nearly invisible in the dark, wet, fogged-in, evening-turned-to-night was a magnificent presence. Light from the foghorns, which Nate had not even noticed, were caught blinking. Gold lights flickered over the computer screen, through the raining mist. The bridge itself, still as prayer.

And Chaucer could not be found.

Nor could the gold leash.

Sometimes I imagine someone running
before me
ahead a few paces, and a few hundred years.

CHAPTER XVI.

PALE LIGHT.

Assia wondered how to begin—the ending, that is—to *November Novel*. She thought most authors preferred that all of their characters be safely "tucked in" by the end of their novels. *Did they?* Or was that sentiment a latent maternal instinct within her?

She knew these characters had started out steps ahead of her, just beyond her reach. That they were pilgrims of a kind. And like the characters in *Canterbury Tales*—the knight, the miller, the nun, the monk—they'd lived lives here, on their own, with one another; she, the follower, the observer, the fortunate one, witnessing as best she could.

She'd not been able to pick them up, hold them, in all the ways she had wanted to be able to... when they were lonely beyond containing, when they loved those whom they could not, when they lost friends, lovers, loves, beloved pets, *a child*—and could do nothing with their grief—could not share it, could not be alone with it, could barely walk with it. And yet, they did all of those things, anyway.

They had played, and worked and worried, eaten meals together, and welcomed new people—characters—into their lives. They'd wondered. And wandered. They'd painted, acted, taught, made art and architecture, and studied. They had worked, and were raising children. They'd zipped through London on skateboards and rollerblades, and had read newspapers on benches along the Thames, lowering the papers just enough to accommodate their gaze, watching two women exchange clothes in front of the Houses of Parliament—a gold and pink skirt, a pair of worn and faded, ripped and tattered jeans—while a gold leash tangled around the leather-fringed pants of a man patting a dog. And they'd taken heart in a newly elected American president.

How could she let them go?

What is the way to leave?

She swept her eyes up and to the side, and thought... *What was it he always said that meant?*

Where was that coffee? Why did it seem others had cups of coffee but she couldn't order one and get it, to save her soul?

She reached down to adjust the turquoise ankle bracelet, the one she wore everyday, which seemed to ground her to something she needed grounding to, and adjusted the fringe alongside the soft leather—wait—the soft denim of the jeans with the violet-threaded peace sign and the tattered rips.

She whistled for her dog, hopped on the skateboard, lifted her eyebrow at the one—snuggled into the velvet couch of the other—

She tried to hold the grief of the two—

She picked up the OBAMA sign—the greens, the turquoises, and the blues—vibrant still through that rainy fall, from the front steps of the brownstone in Washington D.C.—the sign that had been taken down by someone(s), more than once—thrown on the ground—and put back in place by strangers, more than once.

She lifted an eyebrow, in studied consideration...
She needed to send them something.
A message.
Short.
Short as a haiku, for example.
Something... Like This:
> **And why did I think**
> **I could leave you this way, with**
> **-out just one look back?**

All that is gold does not glitter;
all that is long does not last;
All that is old does not wither;
not all that is over is past.

—J.R.R. Tolkien

CHAPTER XVII.

GOLD DUST

Nate was sleeping later than usual. He'd been up until 2:00 a.m., writing, now that he was finally able to. He'd put Neal's playlist on repeat as background, and cranked out an unprecedented 4,036 words on his November Novel, putting him at 43,342. Amazing. More like amazing grace. He hadn't believed he'd be able to catch up and have a shot at completing it in November.

Violette had been soundly asleep on the couch when Nate went to bed, the last embers of the fire glittering topaz, her hair tangling over the pillows. Neal had stayed in the kitchen most of that time, cooking. Nate would never have thought, as much as three weeks ago, that Thanksgiving would find him in the United States, at Neal's apartment—and with Violette. Thanksgiving did tend to gather unlikely, certainly unpredicted, combinations of people. And who knew who might walk through the door tomorrow.

Assia awakened to Stephen's call. "Assia, come with me. I'm going to San Francisco. I'm online right now checking flights. I can't face telling Violette about Chaucer. Maybe I said that wrong. I *have* to face her when I tell her that Chaucer is missing."

"Stephen, what are you talking about? I... I have to get my keyboard fixed, today... the "n" key... it keeps slipping out of use, unpredictably. I hardly know you! I hardly know Violette for that matter—even though it seems in some ways I've known her for a very long time, so much has happened this month. Of course, I have such affection for her... And for Chaucer, as well. But this is craziness! Go, yes, if you think that's the right thing. I can't imagine why you think I should go with you. Here, let me just get myself up and make some coffee. Damn... I can't make coffee here, yet. That tormenting electric teakettle! Oh, for a nice latte."

"Ah, here's a flight that leaves early afternoon, layover at JFK for a few hours—I'll book two tickets and come by around noon."

Assia shook her head as Stephen clicked off. She felt the familiar feeling—excited impulse—that sometimes overtook her, which she usually regarded as a good thing—antidote to her circumspection. Maybe it would be good to get to the U.S. She had no ties to a job here yet, which would shortly become a problem as finances tightened. She could check on Violette, see San Francisco, and soak up some sun and warmth in the midst of the English winter's seeping murk, a damp that she could not seem to get out of her bones. Maybe she could get Aesop to meet her there for a long weekend. Wasn't it Thanksgiving... tomorrow?

Aesop was about to turn in for the night when Assia called. What was she talking about? Yes, of course he could take a long weekend, given that it would be over a holiday. But fly to San Francisco? That seemed a bit much. Why didn't she simply come here? He didn't understand the whole "thing" about this guy Stephen. Stephen... had he met him? Didn't think so. Of course, he wanted to see Assia. But did he have to go to San Francisco to do that? *Going to England is equally daunting,* he thought, tapping his pen on his desk, absentmindedly, varying scenarios scanning through his mind.

Maybe he could use a trip out of here. Come to think of it, the Sunrise Gathering, on Alcatraz, held on Thanksgiving Day, was something he'd long been curious about. Aesop logged-on to check on flights.

Neal pulled the turkey from the oven. More guests were arriving. He'd heard Violette giving directions to someone over the phone. *What could that be about? Did she even know anyone else here?* Nate answered the door.

A woman, a green silk band wound through her hair, stepped into the room. She pulled her jacket off, shaking the misted rain from it. "Ah, it is indeed damp out there," she said, looking for a place to put her jacket. She looked at Nate. "Are you the host, here? I am, as yet not acquainted..." She reached for a hanger inside the opened closet near the door, draping her jacket over it. She smiled at Nate. "Lovely place you have here! Charming..." Her eyes focused on Nate's face, she lifted an eyebrow, "Actually... I think I may have seen you, somewhere, before... What is it I'm recalling? I wonder... Yes! Could it be the ferry—? Perhaps that's it. I believe it is... last night, in the rain. Was it you? Standing with a woman." Nate, listening closely, as the woman sorted through her confusion, nodded toward Violette, standing near the far window talking on her cell phone. "Yes! That is she. I recognize the hair. Distinctive. Indeed. Then it was you! You were snapping lots of pictures, I'd noticed. In fact, I'd be curious to have a look at them—later, that is—if there's a timing that is right for you." She held out her hand to Nate. "Ali," she said, "Ali Myst... and you are?"

"Nate... Hawkins. Excuse me... your last name..."

"Myst... 'M' 'Y' 'S' 'T'—like the computer game that was so popular several years ago. D'you know the one? It's been a dickens of a name—I've had to spell it for others my whole life. Once that game came out, I had a reference for it, for people. A small window of opportunity that it was. You look... surprised, or... Well, I didn't choose that name, you know," she said laughing. "It was already in place. Obviously."

As Nate's watch wound toward mid-evening, Neal's guests were happily eating, Neal too busy to sit with them. The doorbell rang. This time, Violette answered it. Stephen and Assia greeted her surprised look. She'd given Stephen directions, not at all understanding what in God's name he was doing in San Francisco. But Assia? She could make no sense of this. When Aesop arrived in another half hour, she was beyond baffled.

Assia fell into Aesop's arms. "Too long. Too much," she said in his ear. "Let's just move in together. Right now."

"Ah, yes, Romantic-one," said Aesop, looking into her blue-green eyes, "—and live where?"

Neal had finally completed mixing the ingredients of great-grandfather's pie recipe into the heavy ceramic mixing bowl. He grabbed good hold of the bowl and poured the mixture into two pie pans, the oven all set. *What a Thanksgiving. Livelier than most. More confusing than most, actually. A good thing, these unexpected ones—*conversation, greetings, all of that. Yet, Neal had no idea. No idea at all, what the evening would bring.

Violette looked at Stephen. It hadn't been easy for him to tell her about Chaucer. She was touched he'd come to California to tell her in person. She found herself surprised with her attachment to Chaucer, an attachment she felt more strongly since she'd come to California. It didn't seem complete, somehow, to be painting outside without Chaucer at her feet or somewhere close by, his gold leash tied around the easel or around a bench post. Violette missed Chaucer's personality, his lackadaisical interest in passersby, save for those on wheels that came close enough to alert his interest. She'd come to be charmed with his enthusiastic cavortings, when she came home to the too-large house in London that Simon had insisted on. So many changes all at once... leaving Stephen, marrying Simon, moving, Chaucer entering their household. Chaucer had been her solace, her link to the outside world when she'd been living too much inside her mind and heart. A tear slipped, unexpectedly. Much to let herself think about—missing her lively little companion—Chaucer.

Violette wondered if she could paint a picture of Chaucer, and if that would help—or hurt. Perhaps Jean-Oscar would like to have a painting of this companion-in-escapades, of his heart's joy. She drew in a deep breath and sighed. Many losses for her. Too many. Too much uncertainty. Chaucer and his gold leash had linked her to a constancy in life, and in play. What would she do without him?

Violette was curious, spying Stephen sitting across the room, next to Neal, talking with him. Neal was fascinated with physics, she remembered, and was fairly certain that Stephen could satisfy Neal's "layperson's quandaries" regarding this subject. Neal would get a rather long answer to any question he asked Stephen, she knew that much—ask a scientist a question and prepare for a long answer.

When Violette listened to Stephen tossing out terms and phrases related to physics, she imaged colours—even, entire paintings, in her imagination. She'd say, "Tell me that again, that part about the red regions... Something about '... billions of light years in diameter.'" *How could that, at all, be calculated?* she'd wondered. "Is there a... formula for that calculation, *billions of light years*?" she'd asked Stephen. He'd looked at her with bemusement, reaching for answers to questions his students had not come up with.

So hard with Stephen, Violette thought. Why couldn't she ever be with him and just... She looked away, images in her mind's eye. She remembered the time they'd been together, at his flat... The twins had been out of the city for a school trip. She'd stayed at Stephen's, which was all too unusual. That was the time she'd really tried to leave, and found she was not willing—able—whatever the correct word was. As if she were able to separate now. For some reason she had not found that *comfortable and right place* with him. She admired the way Assia could, without compunction, full-out swear when the word seemed to fit. She would like to say: "For some reason, I can't figure out how to leave you. For some *fucking* reason."

Weak. She didn't like seeing herself as weak. She liked to think instead that she tried to live in the nuances, to respect feelings that couldn't find their way into a clear categorical imperative. Celia had struggled with that one, as well. Celia had said a friend leveled this at her, regarding Nate: "The man is married. End of story."

"Just didn't seem to be the end of the story," Celia had said. Even when Celia tried to write that one, that ending. Now and then, she tried. Other times, she gave up.

Violette found that her hardest time with Stephen had been when she asked him if he felt any of the emotional connection to her, that she felt for him. He'd equivocated. Which made it all too certain, for her. *That was clear enough*, she'd thought. Clear enough for her to walk away from him.

The flames from the fire in the fireplace played lazily while the sky's pale light seeped through the windows, and turned to gray—the rain, idling, waiting.

She'd been busy... helping Stephen... What was it they were doing that time she seemed so sure about leaving?... vague images... sensory details... She'd been helping Stephen get the... out of his... after a particularly nice night of...

He was... and she was... An early morning breeze swept through the opened... in his home in London, the angles. . . low—over the. . . and...

"So..." She hesitated. "You didn't answer my question."

"Which question was that?"

"The one... Do you... an emotional connection to me, or... just that you..."

There was an... inflection of doubt, hesitation... that stilled her.

"Oh." She continued to... then stopped. Something... precarious hold... gave way. She gathered her skirt from the... of the bed—pulled it on.

"Actually, it's not... or it's... or not my... What I'm wondering is—if you have felt... before, maybe it's just that you... not... with me."

"It's not that," he said, his voice...

"Then..." She drew in a deep breath, without... pulled on her jacket, zipped it... This was the part she usually did on her own. He was usually... yet, now—he was... looking at her.

... the times she would say, "Ah, just... at this... just look at me..." in some moment of hapless disarray... and he would say, "I am... at you." And that... that way he... while he was... touched her.

He was being his... the same as when she would... as she started to tell him something. And he would... before she could continue. So charming...

But now, he reached... the zipper... her jacket and...

"What does it...?" he'd asked. She knew what it... but her heart was... and she thought she might... if she started to... and besides that, she was angry with him.

"Does it—?" he said.

She shook her head. "Who cares?"

She... and when she got to the... where her... were, leaned over—lifting the tangled heap of necklaces, and the ankle bracelet Celia had given her. She carefully...

He yet stood next to...

"I just... It's not that I... " she said... She knew he did not... and did not so much as... She was otherwise... trying to get out of the flat as... as possible, not... for him, not... with him... What is he—? Why is he—? She twined her snake bracelets onto her wrist, put her earrings in. Maybe he... she thought... Guilty.

He stood by the... one foot in... She balanced her foot... on the...

where he had... and little objects of random... some coloured... in a... an... and for some reason, playing cards...

She threaded the ankle bracelet around her bare... coloured gems ... emerald, amethyst, golden topaz, and turquoise... a sliver of silver linked chain... gems catching morning light through the... throwing crisscrossed... from the light streaming patterns... onto the...

She always... the... traced them with her index finger, and he would say... I know that you always notice the patterns of light, on the...

... her bare foot propped up against the... she said, "...hard... intimate... without getting...without getting all... about you." He repeated that part—the... part.

... smiled.

Her heart...

She... past him, down the... He followed, and at the... of the...

"Hmmm..." she said. She... through the... and into the... reaching for the .... but he was there ahead of her, and pushed

235

it. She climbed into her... She accidentally... leaned over... kissed him...

"What did I do that for?" she thought.

She started her... He leaned into the... "Remember your exit for... 244... you know, yellow and black..."

"244 is not yellow and black," she said. "It is... and..." Synesthesia details.

"Quite," he said. "... is yellow and black. I transposed the..."

"Right," she said. She backed up, just as a... walking a... hit the brake... frustrated with even... waited for the... to... and then accelerated slowly, backing the... out of the...

Only then, only when she had negotiated the turn past his... did she let herself...

That had been the nature of the relationship with Stephen, for some time. She'd separated herself—the emotion of disconnection lagging as far behind her leave-taking, as Stephen's emotions had lagged regarding their being together. He was the one, though, it had seemed to Violette, who then did not let go. Never coming forward enough, never really leaving. Lately, the grief had shifted. She didn't know if that had anything to do with Celia—taking up heart, soul, and mind. It was as though something had simply dislodged from her heart regarding Stephen—not vanished altogether, simply located away, somewhere. She felt a different grief, which surprised her—the sadness of disconnect from someone she had loved that much. Seemed ironic in a way that she couldn't quite understand.

Aesop, Assia, and Stephen sat with Violette, recalling many and myriad incidents with Chaucer, while Nate got that moment

Ali was hoping for—to show her the pictures he'd taken the night before.

"How about if I grab a cup of coffee for you, while you get it set?" Ali said.

"Perfect," said Nate.

"Half and half...? Sugar...? Plenty of it?"

Nate caught hold of Neal's sleeve as he wandered by, coffeepot in hand, looking for guests who may want a coffee warm-up.

"So how d'you know this Ali? Who is she?" he asked Neal.

"Who?... Ali? Sorry, pal—don't know who you're talking about." Neal was distracted, then, by Assia, who was signaling for a coffee refill.

Ali set the coffee beside Nate, *scooching* a chair *closeandcloser* to his, at the computer.

"What's this?" she said, as Nate logged off the setting, and clicked on his photos.

"Hmmm... what? Oh that's the novel I need to finish. Let's see—in three more days. Was just checking my word count. Can't believe I've nearly caught up with it. Need to get started on my 1667 words for today."

"'November Novel'..." she said.

The bridge came into view. "Yeah, how'd you know? Well, I'm not the only one writing it—not by thousands."

"Like This—the coffee mug," she said.

"What?"

"Your coffee cup—NOVEMBER NOVEL COFFEE SHOP // ST. JAMES PARK—I presume that refers to this November Novel you're writing... Where is St. James Park, anyway—? Outside of San Francisco? I haven't heard of it."

"Where'd you get this?" Nate asked.

"In the kitchen... next to that weird little coffeepot. Doesn't seem like a big enough pot to make coffee for this many people... couldn't figure out where to plug in the cord, but the coffee was hot." She shrugged.

"Ah..." she said. "Those foghorn lights... uncannily caught. Looks like they're actually blinking. Right there on the screen. That scent... What is it?" She inhaled deeply, tipped her head to the side and looked up. "Roses! That's it..."

Nate looked at her.

Ali tapped the key on the screen to bring the bridge into wider arc.

"Interesting ring," Nate said. He watched her fingers on the keys, light flashing from diamonds bordering the square blue stone on the ring she wore on her index finger. "... I don't usually notice things like that."

"Hmmm..." She hit the key again, to bring the bridge closer still.

"... Oh... yes!" Ali said, glancing from the computer screen to her finger. "I wear it quite often—an aquamarine... one of my favorites... was my grandmother's."

"Tell me," said Nate, "... She gave it to you, of all of her granddaughters, because... you were the only one who would not change the setting."

Ali looked at him. "That is a charming guess! I can see why you're a novelist."

She stood up. "I need to leave soon... I have a few minutes, though..."

She wandered toward the fireplace, coming to *still* in front of it. Nate trailed her gaze to the painting propped on the mantle. Celia.

"I see why you love... the Golden Gate Bridge, Nate," she said, her eyes not leaving the painting, "—and why you wanted me to see it. Beautifully done. The first rendition I've seen that could capture—the light. Like This."

She turned. Paused. She looked up and to the side, again. Nate watched her. *Lost in thought. What is she thinking?* She untangled the green silk ribbon from her hair, absentmindedly; slipping it around her fingers, she placed it on the mantle in a loose spiral. Captured in thought, she turned back to Nate. Looked at him.

"I'll walk you out," Nate said.

"Okay... Thanks. I'll grab my jacket."

They went together, down the sixteen steps to the main level. She opened the door to the outside, where evening was turning over itself to dark night-sky-blue.

She paused... "You're a good photographer, you know, Nate. The finest I've seen."

She walked down the front pathway to the sidewalk bordering the street. She turned at the iron gate, and looked back at him. He stood on the front step—for at least a minute, or more, after she'd left. He didn't know quite why, even.

Assia sat with Aesop in the kitchen. The entire apartment was warmed from the fireplace's heat. Everyone was well-satiated with Neal's Thanksgiving meal.

"Assia, it's not fair for me to ask you to come back to D.C. if you're trying to do some things in London, for whatever reasons. It's just that... I miss you. I don't want to return to England, I want to be in D.C. And I want to be with you."

Assia looked at him, met his eyes straight on. Aesop had seen that look from her. A gaze across time, long-ago time, long ago into the future time. *How long have I known Assia?* It was a look that meant Assia had come to something all of a sudden that she was not about to back away from. He braced himself.

"You know what?" she said. "I don't even want to try to think it all through. I want... to be married, right now, right here, in this guy Neal's apartment—with all these people we don't know. And figure out where the fuck we'll live somehow, sometime, when we can sort it out. Being married to you is not something I need to sort out."

Aesop looked at this woman, Assia, whom he had loved even before he knew her. Violette stepped into the kitchen just in time to hear Aesop say, "*Okay...* I accept your proposal."

Rain hit the windows, gently, as evening gave way to night. Light from the fire in Neal's fireplace illuminated the faces of Neal's guests who had become wedding guests all at once. One never knew what to expect at Neal's on Thanksgiving. The pastor, Susanne, who was a friend of Neal's friend, Sasha, and who had sat next to Assia while they were eating Neal's incredible turkey dressing and cranberries, was happy to perform the ceremony, on the spot, right there in Neal's apartment in front of the gorgeous oil painting of Celia that Violette had painted while looking at the Golden Gate Bridge—Celia's pale light filling up the room.

The guests looked on.
Assia and Aesop looked at one another.
Stephen looked at Violette.
Nate looked at the painting of Celia.
And Violette had that look, that look of tilting one's head and looking off somewhere, which Celia

had told her that Nate always said meant, "Looking into the future."

Susanne pronounced Aesop and Assia married. The wedding cake was Chocolate-Bourbon-Pumpkin Pie, having just come from the oven, the pie itself pronounced the best west of the Mississippi River, where Neal's great-grandfather had originally concocted the recipe. And where the bride, wearing a pair of very tattered ripped blue jeans with a violet peace symbol stitched into them, had grown up.

The guests left that night, reluctantly. They thanked their host, wished the newlyweds well, and found their way down the steps of Neal's Victorian house into the rainy glow of the streetlights. Neal, Stephen, Nate, Violette, Assia, and Aesop all tucked into Neal's for the night after viewing Nate's night-time photos of the bridge once again.

In the morning, Violette awakened early, before any of the others; she skipped quickly down the steps from Neal's apartment to the main level, letting the door close softly behind her. Early morning light beckoned. Her plan was to gather her painting supplies from her hotel room, and begin her painting of Chaucer for Jean-Oscar. She could do that for him. Violette could picture Chaucer absolutely clearly this morning. *Why is that? Why is it that sometimes we can picture the beloved in full clarity, while at other times we cannot call their image to us to save our anguished soul?*

Those words... Stephen and Neal's conversation last evening. What were those beautiful words? She wanted to put them into her painting of Chaucer—in the colours and textures of the paint on her canvas, Like This: "Light years, bubbles of reality, hidden extra dimensions of space, curled up into a tiny bundle"—*of faith*, she thought, *like a poem, a painting, a prayer—untangling the words love and goodbye—a prayer billions of light years in diameter.*

And perhaps it's Time. To try again. To paint the Golden Gate Bridge—the painting she'd promised Celia, if Celia would finish writing her November Novel. Violette would have to say that Celia's November Novel, left with *mystery*, nevertheless had its own completeness.

Early morning sun poured its heart over San Francisco Bay, skimming the surface through *rays of violet*. The fog would not relinquish its hold, willingly. Iridescent light burned through and, for just an instant, an instant so short that most everyone missed it—except perhaps, the beautiful woman painting at the easel—turned everything in its path to gold.

Nate had not yet decided where he would live.

Violette had not yet decided where she would live.

Aesop had not yet decided where he would live.

Assia had not yet decided where she would live.

And that morning, in London...

Elodie Millieners and Claude de la Ponte, who were reluctantly closing up their house in London to return to Paris, had not yet decided where they would live.

Jean-Oscar, ever vigilant for Chaucer, that dog of his heart, was with Safia on the sidewalks along the Thames—teaching Sir Andre, who had not yet decided where he would live, to roller blade; while the businessmen and businesswomen sat on benches reading the *London Times*, the *New York Times*, and the

San Francisco Chronicle—worrying over the aftermath of the horrific terrorist attacks in Mumbai.

Not one of them glanced up from their papers as a dog trailing a gold leash passed by, on his way.

And that day, November 30, 2008, as Assia and Nate, and thousands of people the world over, logged themselves in and pushed the SEND button on their computers—putting their November Novels to rest, and their fifty thousand word counts scattering into the mystic—like gold dust—Chaucer, his gold leash still firmly attached, settled himself, Like This, on the front steps of a particular flat in London, the place he had decided to live—that *comfortable and right place*—patiently awaiting the return of the author, the writer of *November Novel, by Assia Greene.*

References

Photos/Images

Title Page:
The New Novel by Homer

Page xii-xiii
Golden Gate Bridge: Ellie G. P. Peterson, Minneapolis, MN

Page xiv
Along the River Thames: Shasha C. Porter, Minneapolis, MN

Page 4
Coffepot: ©SlipFloat/Shutterstock.com

Page 16
Big Ben and Bridge: Shasha C. Porter, Minneapolis, MN

Page 23
Westminster Abbey: Shasha C. Porter, Minneapolis, MN

Page 28
Light in room: Shasha C. Porter, Minneapolis, MN

Page 38
"Chaucer:" Marvel Gregoire, Minneapolis, MN
Cocker Spaniel "Daphne Vanilla" resides with Marvel and Jean-Pierre Gregoire.

Page 48
Teapot: Emma S.P. Peterson, Minneapolis, MN

Page 94
"Greensleeves" — Dante Gabriel Rosetti

Page 104
Saint Cecilia, patroness of musicians, by Guido Reni, 1606

Page 132
London Underground: Shasha C. Porter, Minneapolis

Page 150
Study for the picture of Greensleeves by Dante Gabriel Rossetti

Page 188 & Page 191
Alcatraz: Brandon W. Porter, Seattle, WA

Page 203-204
Tom James, Palo Alto, CA

Page 222
Brandon W. Porter, Seattle, WA

Page 238
Iron Gate Detail: ©Bufflerump/Shutterstock.com

Page 244-245
Mark Cross, Minneapolis, MN

Photo of Author:
Elizabeth Lofgren

Back Cover:
Tom James, Palo Alto, CA

Quotations

Page xiii
Paul Klee: (beginning quote) Diary Entry #1104, p. 387
(January/February 1918) The Diaries of Paul Klee 1989-1918

Page 1
Tolkein: *The Fellowship of the Ring*, July 29, 1954: London,
U.K. Unwin Publishers, 1956

Page 85
"It fell. Blue light fell from her pocket in the morning when
she ran in the rain." Source Unknown

Page 95
Greensleeves: Traditional English Folk Song: September 1580
London Stationer's Co., Richard Jones

Page 97
"Are you looking for me? : Rumi: Songs of Kabir, Rabinath
Tagore

Page 223
"Sometimes I imagine..." Source Unknown

Page 227
Tolkien: "The Riddle of Strider," referenced, as well, to
Shakespeare: 'all that glisters is not gold': *The Merchant of
Venice*, 1596.

About the Author

SHASHA C. CROCKETT lives in Minneapolis. Her first two books: *Take My Hand, Twelve Stories of Dissolution and Healing*, and *CANVAS: An Interactive Journal for Healing*, are published under the pen name: SASHA PORTER BLUE. She is currently working on two more collections of essays. *November Novel, by Assia Greene* is her first novel, and is indeed her "November Novel."

25428743R00145

Made in the USA
Lexington, KY
29 August 2013